RECOLLECTION

RECOLLECTION CREEK

RECOLLECTION CREEK

FRED GIPSON

Revised for Young People by the Author

Pictures by Carl Burger

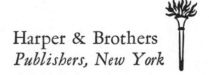

Harper & Brothers
Publishers, New York

RECOLLECTION CREEK

Copyright © 1944, 1945, 1946, 1947, 1948, 1955, 1959, by Fred Gipson
Printed in the United States of America

Library of Congress catalog card number: 58-7764

ACKNOWLEDGMENT

In varied form, some parts of this book were first printed in COLLIER'S, THE SOUTHWEST REVIEW, ADVENTURE, READER'S DIGEST, LIBERTY, THE DENVER POST, *and* THE PROGRESSIVE FARMER.

RECOLLECTION CREEK

ONE

My Grandma Elfie Creech used to have a saying. She said that generally in everyone's life there is a time when he is more himself than at any other time between birth and death.

I used to wonder just what Grandma Elfie meant by that saying. Now I've come to believe what she had in mind was that rare period of living when the days are especially bright, the world is extra new, and the events that transpire are so full of color, excitement, and high drama that, forever afterward, that time is a shiny little gem of remembrance, holding for the one who owns it a special, though often mysterious, significance.

I remember well when that time came to me. It was the year that the drouth drove my Uncle Ike Creech and his family from their Coke County farm, and they came to live with the rest of us Creeches along Recollection Creek. It was the same year that, after we had a killing over a trustee election, somebody burned the Squaw Springs schoolhouse to the ground, leaving us kids free to run wild for one whole term before money could be raised for another building.

Just why this period should have special meaning for me, I don't know; nor am I quite sure just why it should have begun and ended with the coming and moving away of Uncle Ike and his family.

For I cannot say that Uncle Ike or Aunt Minnie or Jay or his big sister Sis was responsible for all the remarkable things that happened along Recollection Creek during that period. Much of it would have happened—in fact, much of it did happen—without their taking any part in it.

Yet there is this to consider about my cousin Jay, who was then a freckle-nosed ten—one year older than me: He was so full of that restless, reckless spirit that grownups like to call "pure devilment" that just having him around seemed to give an

2

added charge of excitement to every event. So it could be that Jay had more to do with bringing my life into sharp focus during that short period than I ever realized.

Looking back on that time now, I can see that Jay often had more to do with some of the happenings that took place than many folks ever suspected.

I remember, for instance, how a few weeks after he came, Jay nearly broke up Shiner Maverick's horse racing.

A bachelor by the name of Aaron Blood was always given credit for that stunt. And while some folks got a big laugh out of how Blood went about it and others got fighting mad, I guess I'm the only one who ever knew that Jay planted the idea in Blood's slow-moving mind.

In those days, we took our bread corn to my Uncle Adam Creech's mill at Squaw Springs for grinding. Almost every Saturday, I took ours. And then after Jay came, he started riding with me, taking corn for Uncle Ike.

Jay brought his corn sack across the withers of a shad-bellied old mare with a ridgepole backbone that he declared would split a hailstone. I rode a gotch-eared dun mule. And Aaron Blood rode a big roan bull.

Blood was a queer sort of man. Not that he looked

3

especially queer, other than when he rode the bull. He was about medium height, a little on the stout side, black-headed, blue-eyed, and slow of movement. He wore the blue overalls and block-toed shoes that dry-land farmers generally wore. He wore the same broad-brimmed, high-crowned hat that was common in those days.

But the way he wore that hat set him apart a little. You never saw a crease or dent in it. You never saw it marred by a speck of dust or a streak of grease or sweat. When he put it on, he took as much time and pains as a woman to get it set exactly as he wanted it. And the way he wanted it was sitting straight and stiff on his head, so low down that its weight generally bent his ears a little.

The really queer thing about Blood, I guess, was his attitude toward other grown folks. I think he hated them. I know that he had no more dealings with them than was absolutely necessary. When circumstances forced him to exchange words with other men, he seemed to resent it. He'd speak, all right, but in a vicious, sharp tone calculated to end the conversation as quickly as possible.

But with me—and with Jay, after Jay came— Blood was different. Not that he was especially friendly or talkative, even with us. But on those days when we were all at the mill and sometimes waiting around half a day for our corn to be ground, he'd shun the men squatting in the shade of the giant bur oaks to come be with me and Jay.

He didn't try to joke with us or interrupt our playing, like some of the men. He didn't even say much of anything. Jay and I could be fishing for channel cat in the pond above the mill, and we'd look around and there'd be Aaron Blood, hunkered down on his heels, watching. He'd be whittling a stick with that big keen-bladed, stag-handled knife he always packed, or maybe picking his teeth with the point of it. And he'd nod a solemn nod, and we'd nod back at him and go on with our fishing.

The roan bull he rode was a gentle animal, and Blood would let us ride him when we wanted to. One time he let us mount and swim the bull across the mill pond. That was a lot of fun; but the other men all came down to see the sight and yell advice at us. And after Blood saw how much entertainment the men got out of it, he never offered to let us swim the bull again.

It wasn't far from the mill to where Shiner Maverick built his race track. Shiner ran a big horse ranch over on the head of Salt Branch, and lately he'd bought some thoroughbred studs and had gone in for raising race horses. I guess it was to get his colts used to the track and crowds that made him want to fix a place where he could hold horse races every Saturday.

He hired men to clear the quick-growth mesquites from the flat and mark out a circular track. Then he put carpenters to work building a little grandstand to hold the crowds.

The Saturday before the first race, Jay and I spent all afternoon watching the carpenters finish the job. A lot of other people who'd brought corn to the mill came and stood around, too, among them, Aaron Blood. But while the others had a lot to say about how the track should have been built and how much money it had cost Shiner and how much more he was liable to make out of the races, Aaron Blood just stood around whittling with his big jack-knife and saying nothing.

Along about sundown, Shiner Maverick and a couple of his riders showed up. Shiner was a big, laughing, loud-mouthed sort of man that we Creeches didn't have much use for. This was because, years before, he'd courted my Aunt Laura Creech for awhile, then dropped her to marry a town woman. Now he rode a cat-stepping sorrel with a white mane and tail. His rigging, a rose-

stamped saddle with *conchas* of hammered silver, was sure something to look at. He carried a huge-lettered signboard under one arm and a hammer in his bridle-rein hand. He swung down and started nailing the sign up beside the entrance to the grand-stand.

Everybody crowded around to read it.

It was such a close-packed group that for a while Jay and I couldn't get close enough to see what it said. Then, finally, everybody burst out laughing and the crowd fell away. Jay and I walked up and read:

HORSE RACES!   HORSE RACES!
Sat., Nov. 1, 1908
HALF-MILE HEATS—$100 PURSE
Entrance Fee—$3
For Anything That Wears
Hair and Runs on Four Feet!

Behind us, an enthusiastic cowhand burst out: "You can always bet on Shiner. He knows how to draw a crowd. I'm going to enter that old Roman-nosed black I been riding. In a scramble as wild as that's going to be, anything's liable to win."

Talking and laughing, the crowd started drifting

back toward the mill, leaving me and Jay and Aaron
Blood. Blood moved up close to the sign, and I
could tell by the movement of his lips that he was
taking his time to spell out each word. He was
frowning some, too, like he was having trouble getting the meaning.

I said to Jay: "Wouldn't you just give nearly anything to ride in them races?"

But Jay didn't pay me any mind. He was watching Aaron Blood. He was watching Blood with that
peculiar light of excitement in his eyes that I'd already come to recognize.

Jay waited till he was sure that Blood had finished reading the sign, then stepped up beside him
and went to digging a bare toe into the ground.

"Why don't your run your bull, Mister Blood?" he
asked.

"Huh?"

Blood's grunt indicated that he was having a
slow, hard climb out of the deep well of concentra-
tion he'd slipped into. He turned slowly to stare at
Jay.

"Betcha that bull could outrun them horses," Jay
added.

"Huh!" Blood said again. Some little something

flickered in his flat, expressionless eyes, then died. He pointed a blunt finger at the top of the sign. "It says horse races up here."

"Yeah," Jay said, "but down here at the bottom, it says 'For anything that wears hair and runs on four feet.' "

"Huh!" Blood said, for the third time. "Hit do, don't hit?" He turned and read the bottom part of the sign all over again. Finally, as if satisfied, he nodded. "Yep, hit sure do!"

Then, as if that had settled something, he got out his big knife, thumbed open a blade, and started picking his teeth while he walked slowly back toward the mill.

I said to Jay: "You reckon he'll do it?"

Jay said: "You keep quiet, Hopper. Don't you say a word about it. Not to nobody."

And I didn't. But I don't think it was because I promised Jay that I wouldn't.

That was the year that I spent a lot of time dreaming of the day when I'd become a booted, spur-jingling cowhand, who galloped bravely about the country, shooting outlaws and snatching fair maidens from under the trampling hoofs of stampeding cattle. And while I did, for a moment there, consider the possibility of Aaron Blood's entering his roan bull in the horse race, the idea was so utterly ridiculous, so lacking in heroism, that I soon forgot all about it.

Also, the very next day was when my Grandpa Vesper Creech had his first encounter with the phantom gobbler that eventually was to lure him to his grave.

TWO

Grandpa Vesper had made a trade with me and Jay. He'd furnish us with a .22 rifle and plenty of hulls if we'd keep the cottontails out of the garden that he irrigated from a spring down beside the creek. Our pay was to be a nickel for every rabbit we killed around the garden. That is, if it had nothing in its mouth. But for every one we shot with a lettuce leaf in its mouth, we were to receive a dime. And if the rabbit had a carrot or beet between its teeth, we got fifteen cents.

As might be expected, Jay and I killed an unusual

number of cottontails around Grandpa's garden that fall and, curiously enough, almost every one of them was eating a beet or carrot at the moment we shot it.

We had five cottontails with carrots in their mouths lying on the front gallery that evening when Grandpa Vesper came in from his turkey hunt. Grandpa had no turkey, but he had one ear torn and bleeding. And he was so terribly aroused that at first he paid no attention to me or Jay or the dead rabbits we'd brought to collect bounty on. So we waited around and got to hear what had happened to him.

Before we get into that, however, I think it best that I back up and tell a bit more about Grandpa. I do this in order to make as clear as possible the strange chain of events that led up to his mysterious death.

Back in his younger days, Grandpa had been a breaker of wild horses for the big cow ranches of Texas. He was a little man, unusually gentle with any horse that could be controlled with gentleness. But for those that couldn't be handled with kindness, he had the wiry toughness, the brutal recklessness, and the bulldog tenacity to bring them under control. He was known to make good saddle horses out of the most dangerous of the man-killer Spanish ponies that the cow country bred in those days. Even I can remember when there wasn't a jug-head bronc on Recollection Creek that could shake the steel-rimmed spectacles on Grandpa's nose. And Grandpa was close to sixty when I was born.

But while Grandpa broke horses for a living, he lived to hunt wild turkeys.

I feel sure that from the start, Grandma Elfie, who was born a Scallon and who finally inherited the Turkey Track ranch along Recollection Creek, realized that she stood second to turkey hunting in Grandpa Vesper's affections. She knew that before she married him. But there was that odd gentleness in him that she'd never known in the Scallon men. There was also his ability to outride and outshoot any of the Scallons. And the combination was too much; Grandma saw her destiny in Vesper Creech.

Too, Grandma Elfie was a practical woman. She reasoned that a man could have worse faults than a fondness for turkey hunting. As I heard her explain it to Mama one time, turkey hunting wouldn't keep a man away from his home of a night, but it would keep him out from underfoot during the day. So Grandma went to work and trapped herself a turkey hunter and a wild-horse rider and never lived to regret it.

14

But there did develop one little rift between her and Grandpa to mar what otherwise might have been a perfect marriage. Grandpa persisted in shooting turkeys around the old Scallon burial lot.

The Scallon cemetery rests on a slight knoll a couple of miles back in the woods from where the ranch house used to stand. It's located on a spring branch that feeds into Recollection Creek. It's in a circular basin, hemmed in on two sides by a curving red-granite ledge and on the other two by towering live oaks and mountain elms. It's a protected spot, and I guess that even today there are wild turkeys roosting in the branches of the gnarled live oak that stands in the corner of the graveyard.

Grandma Elfie didn't like for Grandpa to shoot turkeys out of that graveyard oak. She said it was sacrilegious. She'd ask Grandpa how he'd like for somebody to come stomping around on his grave, disturbing the peace of his bones with rifle fire. She said it wasn't showing proper respect and reverence for the dead. She said that bad trouble would come of it—and maybe she knew what she was talking about.

But Grandpa wouldn't listen. Grandpa leaned to the opinion that the Scallon bunch had been plenty used to gunfire in their lives and had no call to get uneasy about it after death. He claimed that if he were dead, he could think of no better place for his bones to lie than under a good turkey roost. So he went right ahead and got in a lot of good shooting before the day that the first trouble showed up—the day Jay and I were waiting there at the house to collect bounty on our rabbits.

The trouble was in the form of a big lone gobbler, a huge bronze bird with a strain of domestic blood in him, judging from the little patches of grayish white at his wing tips.

Grandpa was squatted in the burial lot when he got his first real look at the wild gobbler. He had his back braced comfortably against the granite ledge and the barrel of his .25-35 Winchester resting across the top of my Grandpa Mill-Wheel Scallon's tombstone. Grandpa was all set for a shot if turkeys came to roost in the big live oak.

But the long shadows crept across the graves, the sun went down, and still no turkeys came. So Grandpa went to work with his turkey caller.

Grandpa called with a turkey bone. All of us Creeches called with a turkey bone. There were some hunters who called with a squared-up green leaf. The leaf was held against the roof of the mouth by the tip of the caller's tongue and he blew on it, making it vibrate like a saxophone reed. The sound it produced was music to any lost turkey hunting its bunch.

But Grandpa never set much store by a leaf caller. He claimed that the only real and natural turkey talk was made by sucking on the hollow bone of a gobbler's wing and for some reason he always seemed to resent anybody who used a leaf.

The old man wasn't surprised this evening when his calls got an answering yelp from the gloom down by the creek spring. The coarseness of the yelp told him he'd aroused a gobbler, so he waited a long, long time before he called again. And then it was just one low seductive note. Grandpa knew how his turkey hens talked to a gobbler.

That one enticing note got instant results. Out of the underbrush strutted a monstrous bird. His tail was spread like a Mexican dancer's fan. His dragging wing tips boomed against the ground like muffled drumbeats. He stretched a long red neck and shattered the evening stillness with a gobble that set echoes to ringing in the basin.

Grandpa's heart leaped and his pulse hammered in his ears. But he held himself rigid. If that was the gobbler he thought it was, he had a job on his hands. Off and on, for the last couple of years, he'd been

17

catching glimpses of a big gobbler with a splash of white at both wing tips. But every time it was only a glimpse he got before the bird melted into cover.

Grandpa knew the kind. He called them "hermit gobblers." They ranged alone. They seldom spent two consecutive nights in the same tree. They changed feeding grounds regularly. They led wary, solitary lives, seeking companionship only at breeding time.

A man had to play it cautious with a cagey old bird like that one; he wasn't the kind to walk blindly into a gun trap. A slight movement, bad timing, or one false note in Grandpa's calling, and that turkey would be gone.

Grandpa waited still longer this time before he called. He wanted that gobbler out in the open where the shooting light was better. Night was almost on him now, but Grandpa had hunted turkeys too long to rush the thing.

It took two more calls. Then the big bird left the brush, approaching at a saddle-horse trot.

Grandpa lined his Winchester sights dead center, pulled the trigger half off, and held it. He'd fire the instant the trotting gobbler halted to strut again.

But the bobcat attacked first. With a savage squawl, he flung himself off the ledge onto what he

MILL WHEEL
SCALLON

thought was a turkey hen calling from the shadows beside Greatgrandpa Mill-Wheel's grave. What he sank his teeth and claws into probably surprised him as much as it did Grandpa Vesper.

The old man's howl was smothered by the lashing report of his Winchester, which he'd squeezed off involuntarily. The startled bobcat snarled his surprise and frustration. He fell loose from his catch and sprang to cover.

The gobbler wheeled, vanishing like a phantom into the gloom.

There was no way out for Grandpa. When he rode in for supper, one torn ear was still dribbling blood onto his brush jumper and ragged claw marks were plain across his neck and shoulders. Grandma kept at him till she got the story of the bobcat's attack, then pinned him down to admitting that he'd been waiting for turkeys at that graveyard roost again.

"I been telling you for forty year," she told him, "to quit tromping around on the bones of my dead people. This here is just a warning. Keep at it, and you'll git in bad trouble, Vesper Creech. You mark my words!"

That brand of superstitious prattle riled Grandpa

Vesper. He spoke sharply to Grandma, the first time I ever heard him do it.

"Hush that rattle-tongue talking, woman, and patch me up," he ordered. "I'll git that big gobbler, and there ain't enough dead Scallons and fool bobcats on the Turkey Track range to keep me from it. And you can mark *my* words."

That stopped Grandma. She didn't hold with a woman's arguing with her man after he'd laid down the law. She held that if a man wasn't fit to boss his womenfolks, he wasn't fit to marry.

She sent me and Jay out to the smokehouse for spider web, while she hunted up the turpentine and sugar. She stopped Grandpa's bleeding and then set out our supper in grim silence. But she didn't eat with us. Instead, she went out to her rocking chair on the front gallery and sat and rocked, fast and long, in the evening chill. It was a worrisome sort of rocking, the kind that gets on your nerves. I guess it got on Grandpa's nerves; because for the first time since we'd been shooting rabbits for him, he acted grumpy about paying for so many with carrots between their teeth.

He paid us full price, all right, but I couldn't help wondering if maybe he was getting suspicious.

21

THREE

When the day came for the horse races at Squaw Springs, I learned a terrible thing. Mama and Papa weren't going! We had a heifer that was trying to bring a calf and couldn't, and Mama said wouldn't people think we were pretty sights, going off to a horse race when we had a heifer dying.

I was filled with panic. I *had* to see the horse races. I was sorry for the heifer, all right; but it seemed to me that if she was going to die, she could do it just as well while I was at a horse race as anywhere else. I was always finding things like birds and rabbits and deer and skunks that had died without my help.

I tried to explain this to Mama, but she wouldn't listen. And I guess if Papa hadn't taken my side, I'd have missed one of the finest shows of my life.

As it was, I had to wash both ears, comb my hair, wear my shoes, and promise to stay up in the grandstand, where the horses couldn't run over me and maybe mess up my Sunday clothes.

I went with Jay and his family. We went in Uncle Ike's wagon. Uncle Ike and Aunt Minnie rode in the spring seat. Sis and Grandma and Grandpa sat in cane-bottomed chairs behind them. Jay and I sat at the tail end of the wagon bed, where we could hang our feet out.

Sis was eighteen, tall and leggy. She had dark brown eyes and long blond hair and such a pretty mouth that most of the time after she came, it was girls like her that I saved from the trampling hoofs of fear-maddened cattle.

However, Jay and I were a little put out with Sis that day. This was because she spent so much time primping and fixing herself up to go to the races that she got us off to a late start.

It was Grandma Elfie who finally went into the house and dragged Sis out to the wagon. "Now,

23

look, honey," Grandma told her. "You can be fixed up pretty as a picture and still not catch a man if you get there too late to be seen."

This made Sis blush and Jay throw back his head and hoot with laughter till finally Sis lost her temper. She said "Shut up!" and whacked Jay over the head with her parasol. Which made Jay mad, of course, and he jumped up in the wagon and headed for Sis with his fists doubled up.

Grandma said, "Get back there, you little banty rooster!"

Uncle Ike turned around in his spring seat, looking angry, and told Sis and Jay that if they didn't settle down, he'd take his mule whip to both of them. Then he popped his whip, and the mules lunged into their collars so suddenly that Jay and Sis both fell flat and Grandpa's chair nearly turned over with him.

Grandpa grabbed at the back of the spring seat in time to save himself and said irritably, "Dang it, Ike, you ain't so big but what I could still take that mule whip to you!"

And the idea of Grandpa's taking a whip to Uncle Ike like he was still a little boy seemed so funny to me and Jay that we giggled about it all the way to Squaw Springs.

It was a fine day for horse racing. It was a fall day, with the air keening for winter and the autumn-tinted brush along the creek flaming red and yellow. The crowd was a big one and gathered quickly, with the womenfolks and kids nearly filling the stands and the menfolks milling around them, talking horses and making bets. The horses were prancey, and their cowboy owners full of talk and good spirit.

Jay and I found perches on the top seat of the grandstand and drank in the show.

Shiner Maverick and four others climbed up into a little judges' stand. Shiner stood up and lifted his hat to the womenfolks and gave them a big smile and made an opening speech. Then he called for the leadoff race, the half-mile heat with the hundred-dollar purse.

Some fifteen cowboys mounted on their fastest horses paid entrance fees for the race, and there was a lot of horseplay and confusion in getting the horses placed and lined up. And before it could all be settled, Jay nudged me with an elbow and whispered: "Looky yonder."

It was Aaron Blood, riding up on his big roan bull!

What with all the excitement and hullabaloo, he had ridden up to the judges' stand and was reaching into his pocket for his entrance fee before anybody else noticed him. Then, all at once, it seemed like everybody saw him. And in the sudden quiet that followed this discovery, his jangling voice was raspy as a raw, chill wind.

"I come to put my bull in the race," he said. "Here's the three dollars."

Under the circumstances, the statement should have sounded merely preposterous. How Aaron Blood managed to make it insulting I don't know. But he did; and Shiner Maverick flinched, as if he'd been struck with a club.

Then somebody's horse crowded against the roan bull and the big brute snorted and lunged sideways, barely missing the horse's flank with a sweep of his long horns. That's when I first noticed that, for a saddle, Aaron Blood had thrown a dried cowhide across the bull's back. And hanging to a rawhide string around Blood's neck was a big cow horn with a mouthpiece whittled for blowing.

The blocky farmer hauled his bull's head back around with a single rope attached to a ring in the creature's nose. He sat there with his stiff black hat bending his ears, still holding up his three dollars toward the judges.

Shiner Maverick's face began to redden like a turkey gobbler's snout in strutting time.

"You lost your brains, man?" he demanded. "Get that fool bull out of here before he ruins a good horse with them horns."

Aaron Blood didn't bat an eyelash. "Your sign," he said stubbornly, "reads 'Anything that wears hair and runs on four feet.' This roan bull fills the bill. Air you taking my money, or is your word like I've heerd tell—not worth a holler in a whirlwind?"

That was insult enough to bring on a killing in those days. I saw Shiner Maverick's hand move toward the pearl-handled six-shooter he always wore, and I sucked in a quick breath, like nearly everybody around me. But just then somebody whooped. And somebody else saw the humor of the thing and whooped with the first one. Then the whole crowd caught it and went to rocking and shouting with laughter, especially all us Creeches.

None of the grown-up Creeches had a lot of use for Aaron Blood. His little piece of bottom-land farm lay next to my papa's place. For years Papa had been trying to trade Blood out of it, and all us Creeches were sort of aggravated at Blood because he wouldn't trade with Papa. But that, and Blood's crankiness, was all any of us had against him; and nobody considered that nearly as bad as the way Shiner Maverick had treated my Aunt Laura Creech when he threw her over for a town woman. So all of us Creeches sided with Aaron Blood and laughed at Shiner Maverick as loud as we could.

Shiner was too smart a man not to know when he was whipped. He'd stuck his foot in his own loop with that fool sign; and Aaron Blood, at Jay's suggestion, had now pulled the loop shut. Shiner could see that most of the crowd was with Blood, and the best thing he could do was pull in his horns. His hand fell away from his gun and he managed a weak grin.

"Well, Blood," he said, looking around at the audience, "I guess you've called the turn, at that. Hand over that three dollars and line up your bull for the race."

The bull made more trouble when Aaron Blood tried to line him up with the racers. The horses kept snorting and shying away from him and plunging out ahead. When the starter finally got them in line, there was plenty of room on either side of the bull.

All the time, Aaron Blood sat stiffly astride his mount, clutching his cow horn in his right hand. He waited till the starter signaled that they were ready

28

and Shiner Maverick drew his pearl-handled six-shooter and pointed it toward the sky; then he lifted the horn to his mouth. Shiner's gun cracked. Blood blew a blast on the cow horn and hooked a rusty spur in the side of his bull.

The bull lunged forward with an angry bellow. He took out down the track with his tail in the air and the loose cowhide flopping and rattling about his rump.

It was too much for the high-spirited cowhorses. They broke and fell away from that roan bull like he was a midnight spook. Most of them bogged their heads and went to pitching and bawling and circling. Three fell down. Five stampeded right through the new board fence that Shiner's carpenters had built, taking their riders with them. One squealing little paint was so terrified that he wheeled and tried to climb up into the stands with the screaming womenfolks.

Some of the riders finally fought their horses back onto the track and turned them loose in the right direction. But they were far too late. Aaron Blood's roan bull was coming around that circular track like a ridge runner. He finished an eighth of a mile ahead of the lead horse.

Blood pulled his running bull down when he

crossed the finish line, circled him, and brought him to a halt before the judges' stand.

"I'll take that hundred dollars," he told Shiner Maverick.

A howl went up from the cowboy riders, of course. They didn't want Shiner to pay that hundred dollars to Blood. They said the race hadn't been fair. They said Aaron Blood had no right to spook their horses with that blasting cow horn and flapping hide. They said that if he was any kind of a man, he'd throw those things away. Then they'd show him how fast his roan bull could run.

Blood paid them no mind at all. He just sat there on his bull, waiting for Shiner Maverick to hand over the prize money.

"Well," he said impatiently. "I won the race. Do I git the money or don't I?"

He got the money. From the look on Shiner's face, it was plain that he'd just as soon have given Aaron Blood his right arm as hand over that hundred-dollar purse. But there was nothing else he could do. The crowd, both the ranchers and the dry-land farmers, had just seen the best show they'd ever hoped to see and didn't care whether the race had been fair or not. They wanted Blood to get the money. The howl and jeering that went up at Shin-

er's show of reluctance told the rancher that. And he knew that no matter how he felt about it, he had to go with the crowd—or risk losing everything he'd put into his race track.

He reached into a cigar box and handed Blood a packet of ten-dollar bills, tied up with a string. "Now take that bull and get off this track," he ordered.

Blood gave no sign that he'd heard. He took the packet of bills, sat there on his bull and slowly counted his money. When he was finally satisfied that he hadn't been cheated, he stuffed the packet into his hip pocket. Then he lifted his hat, pulled out a handkerchief and dusted it off. When he had it set firmly back on his ears, he turned to the cowboys and grinned faintly.

"Boys," he said, "I ain't admitting I've taken an unfair advantage. But seems like some of you don't lose easy, so I'm willing to run the race over. Make up a hundred between you, and I'll bet this hundred that you'll be looking at the rump end of this roan bull when he crosses the line a second time."

That was throwing his rocks straight at them, and cowboys of those days weren't the kind to let such a challenge go. They made up fifty dollars, Shiner Maverick rounded out the hundred, and they lined up for a second race.

32

Blood discarded his cow horn and the dried cowhide this time. He now rode his bull up to the starting line with nothing except the one rusty spur that he wore on the right heel of his square-toed brogans. But when the gun went off for the start, the spur was enough. And the bull was too much.

The truth was, of course, the horses hadn't recovered from their previous fright. The gaps between them and the bull were wider this time. And when Blood hooked his spur into the roan bull's belly and the big leggy creature lunged ahead with a protesting roar, the horn and the rattling cowhide weren't even missed.

We got a better show this time than before. The horses scattered like flushed quail. They bawled and pitched and lunged and kicked and fell down in all directions.

And right up out of that wild scramble, at the most unexpected of all times, Fate handed Jay's big sister Sis what girls her age are generally looking for.

He was a young, slim rider. He had laughing blue eyes and coal-black hair and that bold air or flair or whatever it is that some men have about them to catch and hold the eye of any woman. Sis admitted later that she couldn't have dreamed up a more handsome man nor a more spectacular way of making his acquaintance. For when the fear-crazed black horse snapped Ruel MacLaurin out of the saddle, he rose through the air like a soaring bird to land squarely, if none too gently, in Sis's lap.

He landed partly in Grandma Elfie's lap, too, and had one leg hooked around Aunt Minnie's neck. But, of course, Grandma and Aunt Minnie weren't nearly so interested as Sis; and anyhow, he landed mostly in Sis's lap. Which is where he lay for a good long spell.

This was because Aunt Minnie screamed and went to jumping around, trying so hard to get Ruel's leg from around her neck that she wouldn't give him a chance to get his feet back under him. Then, too, Sis was so startled that she just sort of automatically threw her arms about what had landed in her lap and held onto it till Grandma could get Aunt Minnie quieted down enough for Ruel to unhook his leg.

By that time, there was such a scramble of shrieking women coming to their feet around Sis and her man that I couldn't see what else was happening, so I went back to watching the horse race.

Only, it wasn't really any more of a horse race than it had been before. The only animal still on the track was Aaron Blood's bull, which was already coming in on the home stretch and coming fast. A few of the men just barely got their fighting horses out of the way in time to keep from getting run over as the bull crossed the finish line.

The applause Aaron Blood got this time as he collected his winnings was weaker than before. His obvious contempt for Shiner Maverick seemed to sort of spill over, so that the crowd felt included in his scorn. His parting shot at Shiner was a flat insult.

"Now," he said to the rancher, "you can take your little two-bit race track and go on being a big blowhard. I've showed 'em that you cow people ain't so wide across the britches."

With that, he picked up his cowhide and horn and rode off in the silence that followed his words.

On the ride home that afternoon, Grandpa rawhided Sis so much about the man that had fallen into her lap that Sis finally tucked her face and covered it with her arms to hide the blushes. I expected Jay to team up with Grandpa and really make Sis miserable, but he didn't. He sat beside me in the rear end of the wagon, staring resentfully down at his dangling feet.

After a while, he burst out: "The old stingy-gut! He could have split with us. Wouldn't of won a dime of that money if we hadn't told him how to win it!"

FOUR

I didn't much want to do what Jay had in mind. I recollect how I tried to argue him out of doing what he did before he ever did it. I told him, right there, while we were hiding behind that big clump of prickly pear, that it was liable to get us into trouble.

But Jay wouldn't listen. Jay was too much like Uncle Ike; when he got his mind set on doing something, he wouldn't listen to anybody.

"Squat down," he ordered. "Quick. Before they see us!"

So I squatted down and watched him frown and

wrinkle up his button nose and grit his teeth while he pulled a goat-head bur out of his heel.

The bur came loose; Jay's face straightened; and he went to grubbing in his pocket for a rock.

I looked through an opening between the spiny pads of the prickly pear. Down past the corncrib, I could see Sis hanging on the front-yard gate. Her corn-silk hair shone in the late sunlight. She was telling her fellow good-by.

Jay and I had watched Sis tell her fellow good-by half a dozen times since the day Ruel MacLaurin's race horse had thrown him into her lap. And every time she told him good-by at the gate and then stood there, holding to it and watching him till he'd mounted and ridden out of sight around the bend of the road.

Ruel MacLaurin was Sis's first fellow, and she was sure proud of him.

Ruel was already outside the gate. He was being careful about untying a snorty black bronc horse from a mesquite tree. Any minute now, he'd be riding up the trail past our prickly pear.

Jay got a smooth round rock out of his pocket. He fitted it into the pouch of his slingshot. His face lit up with the sort of grin that always excited me, yet gave me an uneasy feeling, too.

"Uncle Ike's liable to bust our tails," I said. "He's told us time and again that he would bust our tails if he ever caught us slinging rocks at livestock."

"Papa ain't caught us yet," Jay said. "And, anyhow, he don't set much store by Sis's fellow. He says Ruel is a show-off. He says Ruel's a worse show-off than Shiner Maverick."

I tore off a ragged corner of my big toenail and chewed on it while I studied Ruel through the prickly-pear pads. I guessed he was a little bit of a show-off, all right. He'd come up from South Texas about a year before and taken over the horsebreaking for Clell Dawson's big ranch over near Round Mountain. He was mighty proud of his reputation as the best horsebreaker in the country and didn't try to hide it. He rode one of those new broncbuster saddles with a low cantle and a swelled fork. He sported spike-heeled boots with fancy stitching in the tops. He wore yellow batwing chaps and a red neckerchief and a white, stiff-brim hat that he kept slanted across his head at a sort of reckless angle. His saddle and chaps were set with silver *conchas* that he kept polished. Sometimes when he came riding in off the range, he glittered and blazed in the sunlight like a big jewel.

But I couldn't hold any of that against him. To

me, he was all that was fine and magnificent and brave and daring. Give me time to grow up, and I'd break wild horses for a living and sport me some fancy saddle rigging like that.

It was those sporty garments and fancy rigging, though, that had caused Uncle Ike to fall out with Ruel. I understood that. To Uncle Ike's way of thinking, anybody as sporty as Shiner Maverick was liable to be like him. And you couldn't blame Uncle Ike for not wanting Sis to maybe get left holding the sack like Aunt Laura had.

I watched Ruel ease his hand up till he'd caught the cheek strap of the black bronc's hackamore. He pulled the horse's head down and around till it was safe to put a foot in the stirrup. Then, quick and easy as a cat, he went up and across.

The black snorted. He humped up under the saddle and went to crab-walking. He didn't pitch, but he looked like he would the first chance he got.

Some of the other Creeches, who were as suspicious of Sis's pretty fellow as Uncle Ike, claimed Ruel MacLaurin made a point of coming to court Sis on the worst horse he was breaking out. They said he thought it made him look bold and reckless. They said Ruel was the kind who liked to listen to the girls beg him to be careful.

Sis was begging him to be careful now.

Ruel grinned at her and rode up the dusty trail. The black kept blowing and sidling about, hunting hard for an excuse to fall to pieces under the saddle and unload his rider.

He didn't have to hunt long. Jay waited till they were close and Ruel was twisted in his saddle, waving Sis good-by. Then he let fly with his slingshot.

The humming rock struck the horse in the flank.

It was like touching off a stick of dynamite under a mesquite stump. The black squealed, bogged his head, and quit the earth with the saddle skirts popping.

Caught off guard like that, Ruel didn't have a chance. The bronc sent him sprawling—pretty clothes and all—right into the middle of our prickly-pear clump.

Ruel yelped like a scared dog when he landed. He yelped again, getting to his feet. I guess with all the pear stickers he had in him, he had a right to holler.

"You confounded little devil," he roared at Jay; and I don't ever expect to see a madder bronc twister come charging out of a prickly-pear clump.

Jay and I wheeled to run, of course, but we were too late. We hadn't expected the black to unload

Sis's fellow right on top of us like that. We were sort of stunned.

Ruel collared Jay and dragged him across a bent knee. He went to work on the seat of Jay's pants with the flat of his big bronc-buster hand. He sure set Jay's seat to smoking.

I was so scared that I couldn't run and just stood there, watching Jay kick and squirm and yell and gnaw on Ruel's batwing chaps. Jay was trying to bite Ruel's leg, but the bullhide leather was too thick.

The bronc went pitching and bawling on up the slope, loose saddle stirrups flopping high over his back.

Off to one side, I heard a shout. It was Uncle Ike. He was rounding the corner of the corncrib with his hat off and a harness hame clutched in one hand.

Uncle Ike was a little man with a big temper, and he sure did look riled now. He came running up, waving the harness and threatening to cave in Ruel MacLaurin's head with it if Ruel didn't quit beating up on his baby boy. He aimed to do it, too, I guess, because he swung at Ruel's head. But Ruel turned Jay loose in time to reach out and grab the hame from Uncle Ike's hand.

Back at the front-yard gate, I heard Sis scream.

Uncle Ike wasn't nearly so big as Ruel, but seemed like size didn't make any difference to him. He came at the bronc-buster with his fists now, hollering and crying, he was that angry.

Ruel had longer arms, though; he could keep Uncle Ike held off.

"Now, you better simmer down, little man," Ruel told Uncle Ike. "If you'd been working this little devil's tail end over like was needed, the job wouldn't have fell to me."

Uncle Ike shot a wild look around for something else to brain Ruel with. He spotted a dead mesquite limb lying beside the trail. He ran to pick it up.

"Ain't nobody beats up on Ike Creech's baby boy," he shouted.

Ruel growled back at him. "You come at me with that mesquite club, little man, and could be you'll get beat up a lot worse than your baby boy!"

Something in Ruel's voice stopped Uncle Ike. Or maybe it was the look in his eyes. The bronc-buster was sure stirred up now, and his eyes had the hard bright glitter of little glass chips lying in the sun.

Uncle Ike had a big struggle with himself, but he stopped. He stared at Sis's fellow till his chin went to quivering.

"You sneaking, underhanded thing!" he raged.

"Shining up to my Sis and then beating the life out of my baby boy!" His eyes blazed and he started hopping up and down. "I'll get my gun!" he yelled. "I'll go get my Winchester and plant a ball between your eyes the first time you ride into my sights!"

Jay lay in the dirt, listening to all this and letting out a big howl every time somebody stopped talking long enough to hear him. Ruel looked down at him and then back at Uncle Ike.

"You go get that Winchester, little man," he said. "Me—I've got a loose saddle to catch."

Ruel dropped the harness hame to the ground. He turned his back on Uncle Ike and went dragging his long-shanked spurs up the trail, reaching back now and then to yank a prickly-pear spine out of his hind side. He was headed for his bronc, which had stepped inside the loop of the dragging hackamore rope and ground-tied himself.

I thought for a second that Uncle Ike was going to run after Ruel and take a swing at the back of his head with that mesquite club. But he didn't. Instead, he wheeled suddenly, dropped the club, and headed for the house on the run. He was crying as he ran, hollering every now and then at Aunt Minnie, calling for her to hurry and fetch him his Winchester.

Sis met her papa halfway to the corncrib. Sis was crying, too. She caught Uncle Ike by one arm and swung onto it, begging him not to shoot her fellow. Aunt Minnie came running out of the house and tied onto Uncle Ike's other arm. Between them, Sis and Aunt Minnie managed to drag him to a stop before he could get to the house and get his gun.

Ruel never one time looked back. He walked up to the snorting bronc. He yanked its forefoot out of the hackamore loop. The black fell back, rearing and pawing the air, but Ruel stuck a boot into a stirrup and went on up anyhow. Just like he was too mad to care what happened. And I guess he didn't, from the ride he made.

That black all but tied himself into knots, trying to throw his rider. Clear to where I was, I could hear the loud *whoomp* that the air made inside his belly every time he hit the ground.

But it didn't do him a bit of good. Ruel just stood off in his left stirrup and kicked the black in the side with the toe of his right boot till the animal finally threw up his tail and called it quits. Then Ruel forked his leg across the saddle, hooked spurs to the bronc, and they left out in a hard run.

I stood there with my mouth hanging open. I'd never seen such riding. I said: "Gee, I didn't think anybody could ride a bad horse that way—just standing off in one stirrup and kicking him in the belly with the other foot."

Beside me, Jay snorted. I looked around. He was standing up, with a grin on his face and without one tear track on his cheek for all the howling he'd put out.

"Just showing off," he sneered. "But we know better. We know he can be throwed, because we just seen it happen."

Then Jay threw back his head and laughed and laughed. Just like it had all been the biggest kind of a joke.

FIVE

That was the fall that Restless Solomon rented the old Sub Felder place, over in the edge of the blackjacks, and declared that he was settling down for good.

"My drifting days is done," he told my Uncle Wiley Creech. He'd come to ask Uncle Wiley for the loan of a wagonload of corn to see him through till crop-gathering time the next fall. "A rolling rock don't pick up no moss," he quoted sagely. "A man's got to light and stick if he ever aims to amount to anything in this world. Like you and your woman done, Wiley. That's the only way."

Papa was there at the time and knew what an easy mark my Uncle Wiley was for anybody who showed up with a hard-luck story. Papa tried to head Restless off. He mentioned what a starve-out proposition the old Sub Felder place was and pointed out that the last couple or three renters had had a mighty hard go of it there.

But Restless wasn't to be discouraged. "They never worked that old land like I aim to work it," he declared. "Get me a bait of corn inside that work team of mine, and I'll rip the guts out of that sand. Have that old place blooming like the Garden of Eden in no time."

Papa wasn't convinced, of course, and tried to warn Uncle Wiley with a look. But it didn't work. I never knew Uncle Wiley to refuse anybody a help-ing hand. He let Restless have the corn, then had to listen to Papa tell him how foolish he'd been.

"That's corn throwed to the birds, Wiley," Papa said. "A man couldn't grow a wagonload of whirl-wind nubbins on that old Felder place, even if he'd work it. And you know that the first time the sun gets hot enough to burn Restless's back he'll head straight for the shade. And when the weeds start sprouting next spring, you couldn't tie that itchy-footed drifter to a drag big enough to hold him in a field."

Nobody else along Recollection Creek seemed to have any faith in Restless's sticking to farming. He liked to move about too much. He'd thresh a few pecans in the fall, dog-hunt for furs in the winter, maybe chop a little cotton here and there in the spring, then spend most of the summer off on some river, diving for fresh-water pearls. Grandpa Vesper declared that Restless and his little dried-up woman moved so regular that every Monday morning their chickens quit the roost with their legs crossed, ready to be tied and loaded into the wagon.

But I always liked Restless. I believed in him. He'd talk to a boy like he would to a grown man. He kept good hunting dogs and had a lot of good hunting yarns to tell. And around the fire of a winter night, he'd play his mouth harp so pretty it made the tears come, and I'd have to hold back hard to keep from crying out loud, like his hounds did.

It made me proud to see how he pitched into his winter land-breaking. For two whole weeks, he stuck to his farming as close as any man in the country. Day after day, he followed the middle buster that he'd borrowed from Uncle Wiley, singing and whistling lonesome songs or shouting silly things at the dun mule and rawboned bay horse hitched to the plow. Any time Jay and I prowled off down that way, we could hear him.

49

"Get along there, mule!" he'd holler. "Lay yore belly to the ground and crawl up into that collar . . . you bay hoss. Squat and reach for it, there. We got us a crop to put in!"

Then Uncle Wiley got laid up with the grippe before he could get in his winter wood. So Papa sent me and Jay down to see if Restless wouldn't come cut enough wood to do Uncle Wiley through his sick spell.

"Maybe that'll be a way for Wiley to get a little something back for that load of corn he's lost," Papa said. "He won't never get it back any other way."

I expected to find Restless out in the field, following the middle buster; but when Jay and I got there, the field was empty. In a minute, though, we heard mouth-organ music coming from down at the house; so we went there and found Restless sitting on his front gallery, blowing away, while his hounds squatted on their tails out in the middle of the yard and howled.

When we told Restless what we'd come for, he looked worried.

"Boys," he said, "I'd like the worst in the world to go help out your Uncle Wiley during his trouble. I feel that it's my duty as a friend and a neighbor. But I've follered after that middle buster till I've throwed a kink in my back. Can't hardly set or stand.

Was I to take on something as heavy as wood chopping, I'd run the risk of ruining myself, for good."

He slapped his mouth organ against his pants' leg to get the spit out, then shook his head sadly.

"I've just been setting here, blowing and thinking," he said. "Thinking how much money that bad back is costing me every night." He waved a hand toward the blackjack woods that set in just beyond the cowpen. "Yonder's the woods full of good easy money, running loose, and no way for me to get my hands on a nickel of it. All on account of that middle buster kicking up against a stump and jerking a kink in my back."

Jay said: "What easy money?"

"Possum money," Restless said. "Possum hides has gone up to four bits apiece. I'm predicting they'll hit six bits after Christmas. And the woods is full of possums, and I've got the hounds to catch 'em with."

He sighed, then went on: "Man could pick himself up a good easy fortune around here this winter. But what's the use? With this bad back, I'm stringhalted. Couldn't climb a tree to get a possum or chop one out of a holler."

I thought what a shame it was for Restless to lose a fortune, just because he was down in his back.

"Well, look," I offered. "Jay and I could do it. We

51

could climb the trees and do the holler chopping."

Restless looked amazed. "Why, you could, at that!" he exclaimed. "You sure could."

"For how much?" Jay said.

Restless waved a hand expansively. "Why," he said, easily. "I'd do right by you boys."

"How much?" Jay demanded again.

Restless frowned. He looked like a man who was being crowded. "Why, I dunno," he said. "There ain't much to do. Just a little tree climbing and some chopping now and then."

Jay waited, but when Restless didn't go on, he said: "We'll split the catch three ways."

"Three ways!" Restless jerked up straight in his chair, as if his back didn't hurt him at all. "Why, goshamighty. That ain't hardly fair. I've got myself and these hounds and a woman to feed. You boys ain't got nobody. You can eat at home."

When you looked at it that way, it did seem a little unfair for Jay to demand such a big share of the fortune for us.

Before I could say anything, however, Jay said: "We split three ways, or me and Hopper don't go."

Restless looked crushed. He put his harp to his mouth and blew a couple of sad notes, then took it away. "Well, all right," he said plaintively. "If y'all want to take advantage of a pore ole man with a bad back, I reckon there ain't nothing I can do about it."

The hurt look in Restless's face and his put-upon voice aroused such sympathy in me that on the way home I said to Jay: "Why don't we give him half, anyhow? Him down in the back and with all them dogs and a woman to feed."

Jay's scornful glance was withering. "Look," he said loftily, "how do you think people get rich, any-how?"

Having never before given any special thought to the problem of accumulating wealth, other than hoping sometime to discover a buried treasure, I was unable to answer that one. So I let it slide and fell in with Jay's enthusiastic plans for reaping a fortune in possum hides.

We had made plans with Restless to start reaping it that very night, but got delayed through the unfortunate circumstance of my losing three of Uncle Wiley's toes.

SIX

Actually, I wasn't to blame for the loss of Uncle Wiley's toes. But for a long time there, I didn't know that and felt responsible; so that, even today, just remembering it, I feel a sharp twinge of guilt for the nightmare of suffering that Uncle Wiley had to endure.

What happened is that when I reported to Papa that Restless couldn't cut any wood for Uncle Wiley, on account of being down in the back, Papa did a good lot of shouting. Then he sent me right over to tell Uncle Wiley that he'd be along later in the day to cut for him. But when I got there, I found Uncle Wiley down in a mesquite flat beside the creek, chopping away.

It seemed that Aunt Severance had run clear out of cooking wood, and Uncle Wiley was different from most of the Creech men—he didn't hold with letting his women-folks do the wood chopping. So he'd gotten up out of sickbed to come do it.

The grippe had Uncle Wiley feverish and shaky, though, so that his ax strokes were off beat and lacked the whiplash force they generally had. And I'm sure that it was this weakness that caused him, just as I walked up, to let his ax slip and cut three toes off his right foot.

When it happened, Uncle Wiley didn't fall back and shout and howl and take on like some men would have done. Uncle Wiley was a big, solemn, patient sort of man; and I guess he'd let Aunt Severance do the bulk of the talking for so long that he'd gotten out of the habit. Or maybe the sight of all that blood spurting from his slashed shoe shocked him silent. Anyhow he didn't say a word.

And I didn't. I couldn't. I just stood there, frozen to my tracks, while Uncle Wiley bent over and laid his chopping ax on the grass. He did it as carefully as he would have put down a fine-shooting squirrel gun. Even with three toes cut off, Uncle Wiley wasn't taking any chances on maybe nicking the keen edge of his ax blade against a rock. My Aunt Severance always claimed that if Uncle Wiley had been as gentle with his womenfolks as he was with his work tools, life could have been a lot easier for her to put up with. But that never did seem fair to me. I know it for a fact that my Uncle Wiley was gentle with everything.

With his ax safe on the ground, Uncle Wiley sat back on the mesquite tree he'd cut down and eased the shoe off his foot. He was a thrifty, practical sort of man, who wore socks only for town going; so right off we could see the damage. The ax hadn't quite cut through; his three middle toes still hung to his foot by narrow strips of flesh. Above them, the stumps were sure spewing blood.

Still silent, Uncle Wiley got out his pocketknife and cut the strings of flesh, letting the toes fall to the ground, one at a time. Then he took out his snuff can, emptied it inside his underlip, and started working at the bulge with his tongue.

"Now, Hopper," he told me, speaking calmly, "you go get your Aunt Severance down here."

I tore out for the house in a fast run. Sight of all that blood had thrown a big scare into me.

Uncle Wiley's cabin sat on a knoll above the creek, backed up against a grove of tall live oaks. I heard the squawl of a dry well pulley in the back yard, and headed around the house. I found Aunt Severance at the well, drawing up a bucket of water.

"Hurry!" I gasped out. "It's Uncle Wiley. He's cut off three toes down yonder past the cattle tank and he's bleeding to death!"

Aunt Severance stared at me, her blue eyes getting wide and round as an owl's in her lean face. Then she said, "Oh, Lord!" and turned loose her grip on the well chain. She went running toward the house, hollering "Salina! Salina!" in a scared voice.

Behind her, the well pulley started squawling again, louder and louder, as the full bucket dropped back into the well. The chain rattled against the pulley guard and the empty bucket on the other end of the chain bonged against the sides of the well as it came up. Then there was a big booming splash at the bottom of the well, and the pulley quit squawking.

Inside the house, I could hear Salina's light feet hitting the gallery floor as she went out the front way. Salina was Uncle Wiley's grown girl. She was as pretty as a New Year's calendar, with her brown curly hair and big black eyes. Almost as pretty as Jay's big sister Sis. And she could run a whole lot faster.

I turned and lit a shuck for Aunt Dicy Cole's place up on Deer Branch, without even being told. When it came to bad trouble, everybody called on Aunt Dicy. They claimed a town doctor couldn't hold a candle to her.

I was full of worry on that mile-and-a-half run. I worried about Uncle Wiley. Seemed like trouble had been piling up on him lately. Last spring, one of his work mules had just up and died, for no good reason. And the other mule had got a mean spell on and pawed a milk calf in the head and killed it. And then a bunch of Uncle Wiley's fattening hogs had got out through a water gap and taken to the big woods and, so far, Uncle Wiley hadn't been able to locate them. And for better than a year now, Salina had been plaguing Uncle Wiley nearly to death.

This was because Salina couldn't seem to make up her mind which one of the Savage brothers she wanted to marry. One night, she'd have Thurman Savage at the house, courting her; and the next night it would be Silas. And it shamed Uncle Wiley to think that a girl of his would be the kind to cause a difference between two fine and hard-working brothers like the Savage brothers, either one of whom would make her a good man.

Along earlier in the fall, I'd heard Uncle Wiley reproaching Salina about it. He told her then that she was fixing to go blind, baking her eyeballs by lamplight every night like she was, that he couldn't see why she didn't shoot or quit aiming.

But Aunt Severance shut him up right quick, claiming a girl was taking on enough sorrow and trouble when she married, without jumping into it blindfolded.

So Salina was still making sheep's eyes at one or the other of the Savage brothers every night, and Uncle Wiley was still feeling plagued about it.

And on top of all that, now he'd cut three toes off his right foot. . . .

Aunt Dicy's shack was back up in the cedars. When I rounded the last bend in the trail, I saw her old man, Nevershed, sitting out on the front gallery, sawing away at his fiddle, like folks claimed he'd been doing every day since Aunt Dicy married him fifty years before. Nevershed had a bald head and lots of gray whiskers and a bulge in his cheek where he held his tobacco cud. About the time I got there, he twisted his head to keep from spitting tobacco juice across his fiddle, then saw me and lifted his bow.

"Where's Aunt Dicy?" I panted, quick as I could get my breath. "Uncle Wiley's cut three toes off his foot with his chopping ax and is bleeding to death."

Nevershed turned his face toward the cedar hills, looked sad, and spit again. "Hopper," he said solemnly, "don't never marry a good-hearted woman. She'll starve you to a shadder. She'll always be off midwifing or laying the dead out on the cooling board or trying to stop somebody's bleeding. If you marry that kind, you'll never see a fitten meal of vittles on your table."

He tucked his fiddle back under his chin, stared sadly off at the cedar hills, and lifted his bow. "You'll find my Dicy helping Beetle Hood's woman," he said and started playing again.

I was crying a little by the time I reached Beetle Hood's shack over on the next ridge. Partly it was because of Uncle Wiley's trouble, and partly because of the way Nevershed's lonesome music kept trailing me through the cedars, whimpering and moaning at my heels. I guessed a man could get mighty lonesome, waiting fifty years for his woman to cook him a decent meal's vittles.

Beetle Hood came out of his shack to call off his dogs. He wore a lot of bother in his face. Aunt Dicy

Cole pushed through behind him, then shoved the door shut. But that didn't keep me from hearing the groans coming from inside.

"It's Uncle Wiley," I told Aunt Dicy. "He's cut three toes off his foot with his chopping ax and is bleeding to death!"

Aunt Dicy was a big woman. She sagged just about every place she could sag, and her petticoat always had a tag end hanging out from under her dress. But to a body in trouble, there was sure a lot of comfort in her big brown eyes.

She turned and looked at Beetle. Beetle looked at her and then down at the gallery floor.

Aunt Dicy said: "I can't go now, Hopper. Beetle's woman is about to have a baby and needs my help."

Panic hit me. "But Uncle Wiley!" I burst out. "You can't just let Uncle Wiley bleed to death!"

Aunt Dicy looked put out with me. "A body can't be in two places at once," she said sharply. "You tell that Severance to use her head, for a change. She can stop that bleeding with spider web and turpentine, same as I can. I showed her how the time Salina sliced her leg open with a butcher knife. I'll come as soon as I finish with Beetle's woman."

Beetle looked relieved, but I didn't like it. I didn't see how we could get along without Aunt Dicy.

I'd turned to go when Aunt Dicy called me back.

"Where's them toes Wiley cut off?" she wanted to know.

"Why," I said, "I guess they're laying beside that mesquite log he was splitting when it happened."

Aunt Dicy rolled her eyes toward the gallery roof. "Land o' Moses!" she said. "Now, ain't that just like a man? Hopper, you skin out back there and bury them toes as fast as you can. Put them in a box and bury them. If something's et them toes or the ants ever get to them, Wiley'll go pain crazy. Now, git!"

I got. I was already worn to a frazzle, but I ran every step of the way back. Maybe if I hurried enough, we could save Uncle Wiley yet.

The saddled horses of both the Savage brothers were tied at the front-yard gate when I got there. Silas Savage sat on the front gallery, whittling shavings from the post that held up the roof. His brother Thurman was squatted out in the yard, beating red ants to death with Aunt Severance's battling stick. Both of them were long, tall, darkfaced men who didn't waste much breath talking. Thurman was the longer and taller, but he was the younger.

I came trotting through the gate, and their dogs got up off the ground long enough to grin and wag lazy tails at me before they flopped back down. Thurman said, "Howdy, Hopper!" and Silas said,

"Howdy, Hopper," in the same-sounding voice, and I said "Howdy" to both of them at once and went on in the house. They got up and followed me.

Uncle Wiley lay across the bed with his bloody foot hanging over the edge. Aunt Severance was trying to stop the bleeding with a pan of cold well water, while Salina just stood there, holding Uncle Wiley's hand and crying. Salina sure did think a lot of her daddy. I thought maybe that was the reason she was so slow about leaving him to marry one of the Savage boys.

I told Aunt Severance about Aunt Dicy being tied up with Beetle Hood's woman and what she'd said about turpentine and spider web. Then I hurried off to bury Uncle Wiley's toes.

Silas and Thurman started to follow me, changed their minds and started to follow Salina toward the smokehouse for spider web, then looked at each other and finally went back outside to continue whittling on the gallery post and to killing red ants. It was just their dogs that went along. One was a clumsy hound pup, all ears and feet, that belonged to Silas; the other was a big blue-spotted coon hound of Thurman's.

It sort of chilled me to pick up Uncle Wiley's toes, but I had it to do. I pulled a couple of red ants off one and put them in the snuff can Uncle Wiley had thrown away when he'd emptied it. Then I buried them quick as I could in the sand of a dry wash and marked the place with a chunk of clear quartz rock.

Silas's pup Spuddy went up to sniff the place and started to dig, but I kicked him in the ribs, and he changed his mind.

Uncle Ike Creech was unhooking his mule team when I got back to the house. Sis and Grandma Elfie and Aunt Minnie were climbing down out of the wagon and hurrying inside. Grandpa Vesper followed them, but Jay stooped as quick as his feet hit the ground and went to picking up rocks to fit his sling. He looked up at me once, then looked away. I didn't say anything, either. I still don't know quite what it is that makes boys who are the best of companions become suddenly shy with each other in the presence of grown-up trouble.

Down the rocky slant past the barn, I could hear another wagon coming. By the rattle of its wheels, I recognized it as belonging to Restless Solomon. And before Restless got there and got his team tied up, here came Aaron Blood, riding his roan bull and wearing his black hat low down on his bent ears.

I knew that in a little while Mama and Papa would be there, and Uncle Gabriel Creech and his folks from over at Gritville, and everybody else who'd gotten word of Uncle Wiley's accident. Because that's the way we used to do in Recollection Creek. Anytime a body got bad sick or happened to an accident, he could depend upon all his neighbors coming to sit up with him.

I wondered for a minute how come nobody had gone to sit up with Beetle Hood's woman till I recollected that Beetle was said to have Mormon leanings and that nobody would have anything to do with the Hoods on that account. Nobody, that is, except Aunt Dicy Cole. Seemed like when it came to folks being in trouble and needing help, Aunt Dicy didn't have any religion.

By dark, there were five wagon teams and seven saddle horses and mules, along with Aaron Blood's bull, turned inside Uncle Wiley's lots and eating shucked corn from Uncle Wiley's crib. The house was full of womenfolks cooking supper in the kitchen and waiting on Uncle Wiley. Out in the yard, the men stood around and whittled and spat tobacco juice and discussed hounds and hunting and horses and women and the rising price of coon and possum hides and speculated some on the weather. The younger kids were all over the place, inside and out of the house, running and hollering and romping, having such a good time that I wished I could run and holler with them; only I was too worried about Uncle Wiley. Three dog fights started out on the front gallery inside of an hour.

Out in the dark, near the wagons, I could hear some of the older girls giggling and young men talking sweet-talk, real low, and I knew there was some romancing going on. Using the dark to hide me, I eased around among the wagons, listening closely, hoping Salina had slipped out of the house with one of the Savage boys. If she had and if she maybe got talked into making a promise, I meant to carry the news to Uncle Wiley, hoping it would ease his misery some.

But in a minute, I noticed both the Savage men leaning against the front door, as if they were waiting for something, and knew that Salina was still with her papa.

There was hog backbone and sweet potatoes for supper, and my cousin Jay ate through two shifts at the table. But I couldn't eat for listening to Uncle Wiley toss and groan. I kept going to the door to peep in at him, and seemed like every time his face was grayer than it had been the last time I looked.

"It's them toes, Severance," he finally gasped. "They're stuck together and burning like they was laying in a bed of live coals."

Some of the women's eyes popped out at that, and I saw them take in long deep breaths.

Aunt Severance said, "But, Wiley, them toes can't be hurting you. They're—they're cut off and buried!"

A sudden desperate light flared in Uncle Wiley's eyes. "Who says they can't?" he shouted fiercely. "Dang it, they're my toes, and I know when they're hurting. I tell you they're on fire!"

Aunt Severance dodged back, looking scared. The other women all got wide-eyed and exchanged knowing glances. Nobody had ever heard Uncle Wiley be rude in front of his womenfolks before. He was bound to be taking a turn for the worse!

Aunt Severance hurried to the door, where I was looking in. "You buried them toes, Hopper?" she asked. "Just like Aunt Dicy told you?"

I got panicky for a minute, trying to think if maybe I had slipped up some way and not done everything I'd been told to do. Maybe I had left some ants on Uncle Wiley's toes and they were still biting. But when I went back over it all in my mind, I knew better. I'd been rattled, but I'd picked those toes clean of every ant, even the little sugar ants. I could recollect that.

"I done it. Just like she told me," I said.

Aunt Severance glanced around the room with a

sort of hopeless look on her face. Salina put her hand on Uncle Wiley's forehead.

"He's a-fevering," she said. "I'll go draw a bucket of cold water."

She ran out of the house so quickly that I knew she was fixing to cry again. I heard Thurman Savage groan under his breath and his brother Silas sort of growl. Then they both followed her out into the dark to help draw the water.

But if the cold water helped Uncle Wiley, nobody could tell it. His fever got higher and higher, and he talked more and more about how those toes of his were sticking together and burning. By midnight, he was hollering and raving till it was a shame for womenfolks to have to listen to it, and Aunt Severance had to call in three men to help hold him in his bed.

I couldn't stand any more of it. I ran out and climbed into somebody's wagon. I lay down in the bed. There was a heavy canvas wagon sheet lying piled up under the seat, and I pulled it up over me and over my ears, shutting out the sounds of Uncle Wiley's sufferings.

SEVEN

I remember how big, scary, shadowy-black monsters came and hovered over me in the wagon that night, all of them shouting and raving about their hurting toes.

I remember how, after a long, long time, one of them finally seized me by the arm, and how I started up in wild panic, and what a relief it was to discover that day was breaking and it was Aunt Severance who had me by the arm, shaking me awake.

Aunt Severance looked as if she hadn't slept a wink, and I guess she hadn't. Her raw eyes and drawn face made me feel bad about having slept while Uncle Wiley lay hurting, yet I didn't know what I could have done if I'd stayed awake. Uncle Wiley was in the same fix as that heifer—the one that had died while I went to the horse races. Only, somehow, I couldn't feel about Uncle Wiley the way I had about the heifer.

Aunt Severance said she needed help to cut down a high-hanging hog ham, so I got up and went with her. The folks that had come to sit up with Uncle Wiley were still asleep. They were scattered all over the front gallery and the yard, still snoring away. It had been a warm night for that time of the year, yet still cold enough to have some of the folks doubled up and shivering in their sleep.

Aunt Severance and I picked our way through them and rounded the corner of the smokehouse in time to see Thurman Savage's big old spotted coon hound, Tater, sneak through the door, making off with the very hog ham Aunt Severance had aimed to cook for breakfast.

Tater saw us the same instant that we spotted him. He tucked a sneaky tail between his legs and tore out through the back-yard gate, heading for the brush. Aunt Severance hollered, "Drop that ham, you wretch!" and took out after him. I took out after her, and then here came Salina through the kitchen door, waving a broom.

Salina could run faster than Aunt Severance or I, but not as fast as Tater. We were all whipped before we started. I wouldn't have thought there was a dog in the country that could jump high enough to pull that hog ham down or stout enough to run with it. But that Tater hound did it and outran us all three. Slick as a whistle.

Aunt Severance broke down and cried when we gave up the chase and turned back. And when Salina stepped over Thurman Savage, where he lay asleep in front of the doorsteps, she handed him a look that would sure have withered him if he'd been awake.

With the ham gone, the folks had to make out on middling meat for breakfast.

But I still couldn't eat anything much. Not with Uncle Wiley lying in the next room, moaning and hollering. I got the buckets and went off to milk the cows to keep anybody from seeing me bawl.

I was stripping the last cow when I heard Aunt Dicy calling me from the yard. "Hopper. You come here, Hopper."

I left the strippings to the calf and hit for the

71

house on the run. I didn't like the way Aunt Dicy was calling me. On the other hand, just to know that she'd come was a big comfort.

Aunt Dicy's man Nevershed was just settling down on the front gallery with his fiddle when I tore through the yard gate. Aunt Dicy stood in the front doorway, sweating and breathing hard, like she always did when she'd been walking. Aunt Dicy had a lot of weight to pack around, and it wore her down mighty fast to be on her feet so much. She looked down at me and dragged a string of wet hair out of her tired eyes.

"Hopper," she said, "what did you do with them toes of your Uncle Wiley's?"

I had to swallow twice before I could answer. I hadn't been easy in my mind about those toes since last night.

"Why," I said, "I buried them, Aunt Dicy, just like you said."

"Sure, I know," Aunt Dicy panted, "but how'd you fix them for burying? What did you put them in?"

I looked all around. Everybody was staring at me. I swallowed again. Seemed like I just couldn't stand having all those folks stand and stare at me.

"Why, I put them in an empty snuff can," I said. "One that Uncle Wiley threw away. I just put them in it and buried the can."

Aunt Dicy rolled her eyes in horror. "The good Lord have mercy!" she cried out. "What mortal pain the man's suffered due to ignorance. Fresh snuff, a-scorching and a-searing them toes all night!"

I broke down and went to crying then. With all those folks staring at me.

"But you said to put them in a box," I said. "You said to!"

Aunt Dicy came and caught me up in a hug that nearly cut off my wind. "Now, now, Hopper," she soothed. "You couldn't a-knowed. A little old feller like you . . . Now run dig up them toes, real quick, and your old Aunt Dicy'll have them fixed up right in a minute's time!"

Jay and Salina and the Savage brothers and nearly all of the men and boys followed me. But I ran fast and beat them to the place. Then I just stood and tried to die.

There was the dry sandy wash that I'd buried the toes in. There was the chunk of clear quartz crystal I'd used to mark the place. And there was the big hole scratched out in the sand.

Uncle Wily's toes were gone!

The rest of the folks came and stood and looked at the hole. Nobody said a thing. From up at the house, old Nevershed's fiddle started up, and the music came drifting down through the mesquites, moaning and weeping.

Thurman Savage finally knelt and examined the dog tracks around the pile of sand that had been dragged out of the hole, then looked up at his brother Silas.

"It were your dog Spuddy what done it," he said.

Silas's mouth dropped open. He looked around till he met Salina's eyes. Salina broke down and went to crying. Watching her, Silas seemed to just sort of shrink up inside.

Thurman got up and brushed the sand from the knees of his pants. He stood frowning with hard thinking, then said: "Now, he couldn't of et 'em. He couldn't of got the lid off that snuff can." He looked at me. "The lid was on tight, wasn't it, Hopper?"

I nodded. I couldn't remember, but I thought I'd put the lid on tight.

"Well," Thurman said, "it's just up to us all to scatter and search it out."

Restless Solomon shook his head doubtfully. "The chances are sure slim," he pointed out. "After an

74

old scalawag pup's packed it around and played with it all night, that snuff can could be anywhere between here and yonder."

Nobody ever said a truer speech. We scattered out and hunted. We searched that dry wash for a quarter of a mile each way. We looked beside every log and rock and tree and stump. We poked into rat and skunk holes. We moved on up to the house and called on every man, woman and child to come help.

We raked the cowpen clean with the garden rake. We combed every square foot of the yard. We stomped down half the turnips in the garden. We sent some of the littlest kids crawling under the house to search; and Aunt Millie Creech's youngest —the one that always sucked his thumb—got stuck, and we had to get crowbars and prize up a part of the kitchen floor to get him out.

And all that time, the toes we couldn't find were tormenting Uncle Wiley to death.

"You just got to find 'em," Aunt Dicy kept prodding. "The pore soul won't have a minute's rest till we get them toes pulled apart and that burning snuff washed off."

But we couldn't find them. Uncle Wiley's hollering and raving drove us like a mule whip. Old Nevershed's fiddle music kept crying and begging.

But nowhere we looked could we find the place that the pup Spuddy had left Uncle Wiley's toes.

Finally, the bulk of the crowd gave it up and went back to sit on the front gallery and shake their heads. There was only me and Salina and the Savage boys and Jay left. And Jay wasn't really looking any more; he was just standing around, shooting at trees and old buckets and fence posts with his slingshot.

Then Thurman Savage quit. Without saying a word, he just walked off and left us. He went to the house and got Aunt Severance's battling stick. He squatted down in the yard and went to beating red ants to death again.

That started Salina to crying some more, and Silas got mad and jumped Thurman out about not hunting. But Thurman told him to dry up and quit pestering him.

"Can't you see that I'm a-thinking?" he said.

So Salina and Silas and I went back to hunting, with Salina still sniffling and Silas shooting black looks at his brother. But I knew that Thurman was thinking hard. I could tell that by the frown on his face and the way he kept rapping those red ants so fast.

Dinnertime was coming on when Aunt Severance called to us. She needed Salina in the kitchen, she

said; she wanted me and Jay to search the hens'
nests for some eggs. And that's when Thurman
Savage jerked to his feet, like an ant had stung him.
He flung the battling stick to the ground.

"That's it!" he barked. "Eggs!"

He came on the run. "Salina!" he called. "Come
show me where your hens' nests are. Every one."

Salina looked at him as if she thought he'd lost
his mind. So did just about everybody else. But
Thurman didn't let it bother him. He kept after Salina till she started leading him from one hen's nest
to the other. I didn't have the slightest idea what
Thurman had on his mind and I don't guess anybody else did, but nearly everybody left the yard
and followed us.

It was the fourth nest that had been robbed, the
one down past the cowpen, under the mesquite-
sprout brush that Uncle Wiley had piled for burning. Some varmint had located it during the night
and eaten all the eggs, leaving the shells scattered
about.

That was the nest that Thurman Savage was looking for. He shoved me aside and got down on his all
fours. He reached under the brush, among the litter
of shells. What he brought out was the snuff can
that held Uncle Wiley's toes.

Salina saw it first. She let out a little moaning whimper and dropped to her knees beside Thurman. "Oh, Thurman," she cried out and flung both arms around his neck.

Aunt Severance had followed us out. Now she snatched the can from Thurman and went running to the house with it, shouting "Praise the Lord!"

Everybody went to talking at once and followed after her. Everybody, that is, except me and Silas.

Silas stood looking down on Salina, with her arms around his brother's neck, and it seemed like he aged ten years, right there.

"I knowed about that Spuddy pup," he said bitterly. "I knowed he was a pack rat by nature, used to leaving a knuckle bone or a Mexican gourd or something in a hen's nest when he robbed it. But I just never takened the time to think."

When I came out with Uncle Wiley's toes the second time, Jay went to work on the dogs with his slingshot. He sent them to the brush, howling bloody murder. Not a one of them got to see the burying place.

Aunt Dicy had washed the toes to get shed of that burning snuff and packed them in a clean fruit jar, with plenty of cottonseed between to keep the toes

from touching and sticking together. I buried them down by the well and dragged a rock over them, one so big and heavy that I knew Spuddy couldn't scratch it away.

Uncle Wiley's fever was already breaking by the time I got back to the house. The pain had left him the minute Aunt Dicy cleaned his toes, and now he was asleep and resting easy. From the rattle coming out of the kitchen, I knew that the folks who'd come to sit up with Uncle Wiley were back at the table, and I could hear Salina talking happily and urging Thurman Savage to have another hot biscuit.

Nevershed wasn't eating though. He was still sitting on the front gallery, sawing at the coarse strings of his fiddle and staring out across the ridges with a sad look on his face.

I looked in the direction he was looking. Yonder, on the first rise, went Silas Savage, sitting humped in the saddle, like it hurt him to ride. His pup Spuddy was following at his horse's heels. And trailing them all, was Nevershed's fiddle music, low and lonesome.

I was hungry now, but I stood there and watched till Silas rode out of sight. And I wondered what there was about a man with a coon hound big enough to pack off a whole hog ham that made him better for marrying than his twin brother who owned an egg-sucking pup.

Finally, I decided that nobody except Salina could answer that one and probably she wouldn't. So I went into the kitchen, where I slipped in on the bench beside Jay and went to eating hog backbone and sweet potatoes out of his plate.

EIGHT

We Creeches took considerable pride in the fact that Uncle Ike could get the maddest, the quickest, of anybody in our part of the country.

In fact, it is entirely possible that in talking so much about Uncle Ike's hair-trigger temper, we built him a reputation that he often found hard to live up to. Especially the part about his anger cooling as quickly as it flared and about his never holding a grudge.

For the truth is that after he got so mad at Ruel MacLaurin that day for spanking Jay, Uncle Ike not only held a grudge, but seemed to nurse it. He packed a Winchester everywhere he went and let it be known that he was just aching for the chance to line up his sights on that smart-aleck bronc twister.

This worried Aunt Minnie, and she did a lot of talking to Uncle Ike, trying to convince him that he was wrong. She said that just because Sis's fellow had lost his temper and given Jay a thrashing, that didn't make it a killing matter.

"That wretched Jay," she said, "he had a good spanking coming to him."

"Not from no high-handed bronc rider, he didn't," Uncle Ike flared. "Never knowed a bronc rider yet what didn't like to think he was the biggest turtle in the puddle. Always throwing their weight around, like farmers was dirt under their feet."

"Your daddy was a horsebreaker," Aunt Minnie reminded him.

"That was back in the old days," Uncle Ike argued. "And anyhow, Pa wasn't no pretty boy."

"Ruel MacLaurin ain't no pretty boy, either," Aunt Minnie defended. "He's just a fine-looking young man that Sis can feel lucky to have for her fellow."

That remark made Uncle Ike's face turn black. He stood up and pounded the kitchen table with his fist, setting the dishes to jumping and rattling.

83

"Fine looking!" he raged. "Now, ain't that just like a woman? See a bunch of fancy trappings and go blind as a bullbat in the hot sun. Hang tassels on a sway-backed jackass, and you can bet some fool woman would call him a race horse. I tell you a man who'll beat up on a pore little old defenseless baby boy—why, it'd be a disgrace for our Sis to be seen with him!"

He lifted his fist and whammed the table again. "And you can depend upon this; Ike Creech has got the sense and the gall to keep a black-hearted scoun'l like that drove from his door!"

Aunt Minnie tried hard, but she couldn't change Uncle Ike's way of thinking. He was bent on planting a rifle ball between Ruel MacLaurin's eyes the first time that fancy-rigged scissorbill rode within gun range.

Sis stayed out of the arguments. All she did was droop around the house, like a sick chicken, quiet as a shadow, looking peaked and sad, ready to go off and cry anytime Uncle Ike mentioned shooting her fellow.

I felt sorry for Sis. I didn't want Ruel MacLaurin killed and I didn't want Uncle Ike to do the killing. I wished things were back like they were at first. I wished Ruel's wild horses were still stomping out holes around the front-yard gate. I wished Ruel was still coming to sit on the front gallery and spin his spur rowels with his fingers while he courted Sis. I missed Ruel bad. Especially the sight of his pretty cowhand garments and fancy saddle rigging.

Within a couple of weeks, however, I was beginning to miss Sis, too. I began to notice that nearly every time I dropped in to visit Jay, Sis would be gone sometime during the day, often for as long as a couple or three hours at a time. And I noticed that when she was at the house, the color was back in her face and she was able to eat well and regular again. Sometimes she'd even sing some while she washed the dishes.

Uncle Ike took note of it and spoke to Aunt Minnie about it, real pleased. "Our girl Sis ain't nobody's fool," he bragged to Aunt Minnie. "She's done seen how right her papa can be and is content to let that bronc twister peddle his fancy goods some place else."

Aunt Minnie let him talk and didn't answer a word, but I couldn't help noticing that at such times she wore a curiously smug look on her face. And I noticed, too, that when she and Sis thought nobody else was around, they often carried on a lot of excited talking and laughing. They were mighty quiet about it, too quiet, in fact, so that it was plain they were enjoying some happy secret that they were bent on keeping to themselves.

I didn't have any idea what it was all about, but I can remember how disappointed I was in Sis. To me, it didn't seem quite right for Sis to forget her fellow so quickly that she could already be joking and laughing with her mama like she was.

Then it wasn't long till I learned that she hadn't forgotten Ruel MacLaurin at all.

It was an extra warm day in January, like we sometimes get in Texas. Jay and I had rabbit-hunted down to Grandpa Vesper's dirt tank in the back side of the pasture. We had sat down on the dump to rest and got to looking at the water and thinking how hot we were and how cool the water looked. And the next thing we knew, we'd stripped off our clothes and jumped in.

Well, the first plunge nearly took our breaths, and the goose pimples broke out all over us. But, after that, the water didn't seem too awful cold. So we paddled around awhile and then got out to have us a mud fight. And Jay had just finished spattering me in the face with a big water-soaked cow chip when Uncle Ike rode up on a horse and caught us.

Uncle Ike didn't like it a bit. He told us to get

right out of that nasty place and stay out. He said this wasn't the time of the year for swimming.

"And don't let me catch you all sneaking off down to that old baptizing hole, either," he wound up. "That hole is deep and dangerous. Brother Wiley claims that Parson Shaffer come within an inch of drowning a backslider in that hole during the revival last summer."

So Jay and I put on our clothes and did exactly what Uncle Ike told us. We went to a good bit of trouble to keep him from catching us sneaking off down to the baptizing hole.

It was a big wide pothole, just below a sand-rock ledge that cut across Recollection Creek. The floods spilled over the ledge and kept the hole washed out deep in the coarse brown sand. There was a high dirt bank on the north, with pole elms and live oaks growing on top and a seep spring coming out from under their roots. The seep spring fed the pool and kept it full of clean clear water, even in the driest times.

We approached the pool from the south bank. It was low and thickly matted with winter grass, so that our feet made no sound. And that's where we found Jay's sister Sis. She sat with her back against a boulder and was all cuddled up in a tight hug with Ruel MacLaurin.

A bronc horse of Ruel's was staked out on a long picket rope. He had cropped to the ground just about all the grass the rope would let him reach, so I knew that Sis and Ruel had been there, hugging each other, for a good long spell.

Jay and I stopped the instant we saw them. Jay motioned to me, and we sank to the ground. We crawled closer, then sat up on our heels behind a bristling turkey-pear bush, where we couldn't be seen.

Sis had her head nestled down against Ruel's shoulder. Her face was all pinked up, and she was arguing. "But you know I do, Ruel," she was saying. "It's just that I don't know what to do about Papa. It'd break Papa's heart for us to run off, like that."

I couldn't hear what Ruel said, but whatever it was made Sis sit up suddenly and shake her finger in his face.

"Now, you hush that kind of talk," she ordered. "I know Papa's hot-headed and stubborn. Just like you. You're both so high-handed and touchy that nobody with any sense would try to reason with you. That's why we're in this fix."

That's when the bronc threw up his head and

snorted. His ears were bent straight toward me and Jay.

Sis came instantly to her feet. She caught sight of me and Jay behind the turkey-pear bush and cried out, "Oh, my goodness, it's Jay!"

Jay cut to run, and Sis said in a scared voice: "Catch him, Ruel. Hurry and catch him, or he'll tell Papa."

Jay took to the brush like a scared rabbit. I skinned out after him.

We got a good head start on Ruel before he could untie his bronc horse and mount. After that, though, it was no use. We heard the brush popping behind us and the sound of the horse's hoofs pounding the turf. Here came Ruel, spurring past me and moving up beside Jay. Without checking the speed of his running horse, Ruel leaned far out of the saddle and grabbed Jay by the seat of his pants. He lifted him, squawling and kicking, and laid him across the saddle in front of him. Like packing a dogie calf. He circled his horse and rode back toward Sis, laughing loud at the fight Jay put up to get loose.

There wasn't any use in my running any longer, so I turned and followed them. Ruel dumped Jay to the ground in front of Sis and sat in his saddle, grinning, while Jay glared up at him.

"Jay, please!" Sis begged. "You mustn't tell Papa."

"Why not?" Jay demanded.

"Why," Sis said, "because Papa might shoot him."

"*Might*," Jay said. "You know doggone well Papa will shoot him."

Sis looked horrified. Her eyes got wide and her breath came hard. "But Jay," she said, "don't you care?"

Jay sneered at her. "It don't make me no never-mind what Papa shoots," he said.

He looked up at Ruel. To see how the bronc-buster would take that remark, I guess. But Ruel didn't seem to notice. He was licking the paper edge of a cigarette he'd just rolled and seemed to be making a close study of the treetops across the pool.

Sis stamped her foot. "Now, you listen to me, Jay Creech!" she said.

Jay grinned that grin of his. "All right," he said. "I'll listen. If I get enough out of it."

Sis's blue eyes blazed, then the fire died. "I might have known how it would be," she sighed. "What's the price?"

Jay wrinkled his forehead, thinking hard. "Well," he said, "I'm getting awful tired of slopping Papa's meat hogs so regular."

"I'll slop the hogs," Sis said.

"And me and Hopper, here, we don't get half enough sugar muffins."

"I'll make all the muffins we've got sugar for."

"Then I'm needing some money," added Jay, "for a .22 target gun and about five boxes of hulls. And I could use an agate marble taw and—"

"But I can't," Sis broke in. "Where would I get money for all those things?"

Jay jerked a thumb toward Ruel. "He's got money, I bet. Been breaking horses steady, all year long. He's bound to have a pile of money."

Sis turned a hopeless look up toward her fellow.

Ruel studied the burning end of his cigarette a little bit before he grinned. "Best I can add it all up," he said, "it'd be a heap cheaper to run off, like I been wanting."

Sis's face turned white and her bottom lip started quivering.

Ruel's grin played out. He quit his saddle and went to slip an arm around Sis. "Now, don't do that, honey," he begged, worried. "I was just hoorawing. You slop the hogs and make the muffins. I'll foot the bill for the rest. We'll try to make out till we can get your daddy to seeing things different."

"We'll make out," Jay said, "if you're here with that money tomorrow."

Ruel's face got hot. For a second there, I thought he was going to grab up Jay and give him another thrashing, like he'd done the first time. Jay started backing up, looking wary.

Then Ruel took a deep breath and let it out slowly. "I'll be here," he promised Jay. "Right about this time of the day."

That satisfied Jay. He winked at me and grinned. "All right, Hopper," he said, "I guess we can go swimming now." And he started shucking out of his clothes, right there in front of them.

Sis's face turned red and she started in a run for the brush, with Ruel following and leading his horse.

"I could kill him!" Sis raged. "I could just murder him!"

Ruel threw back his head and laughed. "Now, simmer down, honey," he called after her. "That sounds too much like the way your papa talks."

NINE

Restless Solomon was careful to keep a close check on the almanac; he wanted the signs to be exactly right for our fortune-making venture into possum hunting.

When the right time came, he sent us word, and we grabbed up an ax and a coal oil lantern and set out for his house.

We arrived there just after dark. Restless was out in the yard, waiting. As soon as he heard us coming, he shouted an eager welcome and blew a blast on the goat horn he used to call his dogs. The horn had a high note that brought the hounds to him on the run, baying loud and lonesome. It also set my blood to humming in my veins.

"We're sure lucky," I told Jay, "to get the chance to make so much out of possum hunting. Most people have to work for money."

Jay said wisely: "Nobody ever made a fortune out of work."

Restless led us toward the post-oak hollow back of his house. It was full dark now, with a little cantaloupe rind of a moon hanging high up among the stars. Dew was already falling. There would be frost in the low places by morning. You could tell that by the nippy feel of the air. It sure seemed like a good possum-hunting night. I guessed I'd buy me a good horse and saddle out of my share of our first night's catch.

There were no possums in the post-oak hollow. We hunted all through it and clear out on the china-ball ridge on the other side. The black-and-tan hounds, Brag and Cindy, worked it close, too. The three half-grown pups mostly just romped around; but Brag and Cindy got right down to business from the start, sniffing for possum scent every step they took. Seemed like they couldn't help but start a possum trail in that post-oak bottom, but they didn't do it.

I was disappointed, but Restless wasn't.

95

"We was just overanxious and got out ahead of the possums," he said. "Let's hit for them rocks the yonder side of Deer Creek. There was a good crop of black persimmons in them rocks this fall. Time we make it there, possums will be feeding all over them bushes."

Straight through, it was a four-mile walk to the rocks the yonder side of Deer Creek. But Restless had some little side trips he wanted to make—one to a cattle tank in Aaron Blood's pasture and another to a grapevine-hung thicket of live oak up the slant of Wildcat Hill. He said he'd be willing to bet good money we'd jump possums in both those places.

But we didn't.

"Our luck'll change, once we hit that persimmon country," Restless declared. "One time me and Clyde Manning takened a round dozen possums out of them rocks before midnight. Big old possums, too."

I hoped the dozen we caught there would all be big ones.

We finally made it to the rocks. They were big sandstone rocks. They stood up on their edges and all leaned in the same direction. In between the rocks grew the persimmon bushes. The bushes were thick and still had some shriveled black persimmons on them. It was sort of wild and scary looking, there among those rocks and bushes. It sure looked like a good place to hunt possums.

Brag and Cindy went to work in the pale moonlight. They sniffed around the rocks and under the bushes. Pretty soon, Brag wrung his tail and let out a long, singing trail bark. Cindy hurried over to smell the place. She stood and wrung her tail and bawled, too.

Restless threw up his head and said, "Hup! Hup! Like I told you, things is fixing to pick up, here in these persimmon bushes."

The dogs circled the place. They worked slow and careful. They sniffed hard among the leaves. They circled wider and tried harder. But they never could locate another scent worth a second bawl.

"Trail's too cold," Restless said. "That fool possum's bound to've quit his bed before sundown. We just got here a little late."

We wandered all around through the uptilted rocks. We crossed a high hogback ridge and hunted down the opposite slope. Here the rocks stood on edge and leaned in a different direction. But there were no possums among them either.

It was a good long while before it finally came to Restless why we couldn't catch any possums among the slanted rocks and persimmons.

"It's them plague-taked Savage boys," he said.

"They been hunting in here, regular, with that old Tater hound. Started before possum hides was prime. Forgot all about it. Feller gets old and down in the back, like me, he ain't fit for recollecting nothing."

He stood and stared off across the dark ridges, looking thoughtful. Jay and I sat down on a rock.

"Why don't you sit down and rest your back?" Jay said.

Restless turned his head quickly. "Don't never do that," he said sharply.

"Do what?" I said.

"Sit down, while you're possum hunting," Restless said. "You'll cool off too quick in this night air. Take double pneumonia and die. Then look what a pickle you're in."

We got up quickly. It sure had felt restful, sitting on that rock; but, of course, we didn't want to take double pneumonia and die.

Restless led off toward the moon rind that was now hanging low in the crotch of some hills to the west. "I've possum-hunted for years," he said. "Longer than most. Always found it a heap safer to keep up a sweat."

We kept up a sweat from there to Red Hill where Restless said that the winter before Brag and Cindy had treed seven possums up one tree. It was a long haul, but I guessed it would be worth it to put seven possums up one tree.

The moon was nearly down when we got there. We crossed a wide patch of grass burs growing in an old laidout field. We reached the foot of Red Hill and stood in the dark under some big oaks, listening for the hounds to cut loose on a hot trail.

Jay listened for a while, then took a chance on contracting pneumonia and sank to the ground. "Why, I can't even hear the dogs," he said.

"They're wide hunters," Restless said with pride. "I better call them in before they hit a hot trail and take it clear out of hearing."

He blew a long blast on his goat horn. Then he cupped a hand behind one ear to help his listening.

The dogs answered him right back. They were behind us, just the other side of the old laid-out field we'd crossed. When they heard the horn, they went to whimpering and howling and crying, like lost babies.

"Plague take it!" Restless said. "They're stuck up in them grass burs." He started back across the clearing. "We just as well go tote 'em across," he said. "You can't expect dogs to catch a possum when they're wading belly-deep in grass burs."

99

On account of Restless's bad back, Jay and I did the toting.

Carrying the pups across the grass burs wasn't so bad; they were small and light. But when I loaded Brag across my shoulder, it seemed like the dark fringe of timber we were headed for kept moving off. I had no idea a possum hound could get to weighing so much after you'd carried him a couple hundred yards.

Jay and I were staggering and sweating and gasping for breath when we finally set the hounds down.

But Restless didn't seem to notice. "Reckon we'll be forced to visit that dead heifer in your daddy's pasture," he said to me. "You can always strike a possum trail around a dead cow."

It was a five-mile walk to where the dead heifer lay in Papa's pasture, but Restless traveled with a long-reaching step that was surprising for a man down in his back. We made it in less than an hour.

The moon was completely down now. The darkness was so black that you couldn't see where to spit. But we didn't have any trouble locating the dead heifer.

The closer we got to the heifer, the riper she smelled. Restless kept going toward her, however, till I was nearly gagging.

Jay pinched his nose shut with his fingers, so that he talked like he had a bad cold. "Ain't this close enough?" he said.

"Aw, just lick the tip ends of your fingers and wet your nostrils with them," Restless said. "That'll take the scent clear away."

Jay and I licked the tip ends of our fingers and wet our nostrils, but it didn't take the scent away.

All of a sudden, Brag blasted the dark with a rousing bawl.

"Hup! Hup!" Restless exclaimed. "Like I said—you can always pick up a possum trail around a dead cow."

Cindy came tearing through the dark. She opened where Brag had, telling it loud and eager. Brag bawled again. The pups fell in, screeching and squawling louder than they did when Restless's woman tried to beat them out of the slop bucket.

"Why, they've got him in sight!" Restless declared. "Bound to have. They don't bark like that when they're just trying to make a hot trail out of a cold one."

A minute before, I'd been so tired that it seemed like I couldn't take another step. Now I was as excited as the pups. Looked like we were getting started on making that fortune, after all!

Restless slapped me and Jay on our backs. "Listen to that!" he exclaimed. "Did you ever hear a prettier sound?"

"It's sure pretty, all right," I agreed.

"Prettiest sound God ever made," Restless declared. "I tell you now—when my dying time comes, there's just one thing I want buried with me. A possum hound. Just let me land on the Other Side with a sweet-mouthed possum hound, and they can throw all them golden harps in the river."

The trail swung left and led off across a mesquite flat. Restless said "Hup! Hup!" again and set out after the dogs in a swinging trot. Jay and I trotted after him.

We crossed the flat and a rocky ridge on the other side, then went down into a creek bottom. The chase got faster and louder. We quit trotting and went to running.

Restless hollered back over his shoulder. "That can't be no possum they're after. They was talking possum at the start, but can't no possum run off like this from Brag and Cindy. Them's the fastest possum dogs in the country."

"You figure it's a fox?" I panted.

"Fox or a wolf," Restless said. "Some kind of big, fast-running varmint they ain't used to running."

"What'll a fox or wolf hide bring?" Jay wanted to know.

"Ain't for certain what them hides is quoted at," Restless said. "But they'll bring a-plenty."

We ran through a tangle of saw briers that tripped and threw me twice and Jay once. We tore through a bluethorn thicket. Restless brushed aside a thorny branch and let it swing back just in time to slap me in the face. The bite of those stinging thorns made the tears come to my eyes and the goose pimples pop out all over my hide. We went through some more rock country, and it was too dark to see the rocks. We tripped over them and fell down, skinning our shinbones from our ankles to our knees.

That is, Jay and I did. Restless never tripped one time. I didn't see how a man with a bad back could get through those rocks so quickly, but Restless drifted through as easily as the hounds.

We hand-climbed a high ledge and waded cold creek water three times. Once Jay got trapped in a soap hole where the slime was waist deep. The mud sucked around him so tight that we had to catch hold of his hands and pull him out.

We were wet and worn out and skinned from head to foot by the time the dogs barked treed.

They had treed their quarry up one of the biggest elm trees in the bottom. We lit the lantern and held it high, trying to shine the varmint's eyes. The tree was so tall that the light reached only up to the lowest branches. We couldn't see a thing.

Restless stood scratching his head and studying. "Now, it can't be a coon," he said, "because them dogs wasn't talking coon. And it can't be a wolf, because a wolf can't climb a tree. And the chances are all agin a fox ever picking such a straight-up tree to climb. So here we are with a bobcat."

"What's a bobcat worth?" Jay wanted to know.

I stared up at the tall straight trunk of the elm. There wasn't a handhold on it for the first twenty feet up. "That tree's going to be hard to climb," I said.

"Climb!" exclaimed Restless. "Boy, we can't risk climbing that tree. Too dangerous. Jump yourself a Mexican lion up in that dark, and he'd have your eyeballs clawed out before you could turn loose and fall."

That scared me. I sure hadn't thought about maybe having a Mexican lion treed.

"Well, how'll we ever get him out?" I asked.

"Why, that'll be pickings," Restless said. "We'll just chop that tree down and turn the rascal over to the dogs."

I looked at the elm trunk again. It was about three feet thick, it looked like.

Jay was looking at the size of the tree trunk, too. He asked Restless how much the hide of a Mexican lion would sell for, but Restless didn't seem to hear him.

"I'll hold the light," Restless said, "while you boys tie into that tree with a chopping ax. Won't take no time to lay that tree on the ground."

I thought it would take some longer than that, but I guessed that when you had a fortune up a tree you couldn't hardly just go off and leave it sitting there.

That old elm was sure a tough one. Even worse than I'd thought. The wood was snarly and knotty and cross-grained. I couldn't seem to break out a chip, no matter how I slanted my ax strokes. I whacked and I hewed. The sweat poured and my legs started trembling.

When my breath gave completely out, I turned the ax over to Jay. He chopped till he gave out, then handed it back to me.

"You're doing fine, boys!" Restless encouraged. "Wasn't for my old back, I'd spell you. But when a man gits old and down in the back, he ain't able to have no real fun any more."

The east was graying for daylight and there was a spot under my shoulder blade burning like a coal of fire when I finally heard the wood crack. I ducked back to let the tree fall. The cut Jay and I had made looked like where a couple of beavers had been gnawing, but the elm was ready to fall at last.

It fell slow, at first, then came down fast and hard, with branches popping and cracking against the ground.

Restless yelled at the top of his voice. The hounds rushed in among the broken branches, baying loud.

"Keep back, boys," Restless shouted in warning. "You get caught in a lion-and-dog fight and you're liable to get chawed up bad!"

The hounds charged back and forth through the elm branches. They pulled off and circled the fallen tree a time or two in a fast run. Then they slowed down and hushed their excited barking.

"Plague take it!" Restless said. "It must've jumped off onto another tree."

He lifted the lantern high and started circling another elm that stood close by. This elm looked even bigger at the bottom than the first. I looked at Jay and he looked back at me, but we didn't either one say what we were thinking.

Then I heard a rustle in the fallen elm top behind us. Brag rushed in and started barking. Restless came running back with the lantern. He held it up high.

There sitting on a branch that was just out of jumping reach of Brag was a possum. It was the littlest possum I ever saw. It didn't look any bigger than a starved rat. It was sitting there with its tail curled around a branch, blinking at the light.

Restless was flabbergasted. He stood and stared with his mouth hanging open. "Well, would you look at that!" he finally managed to say.

He turned to me and Jay. "I never seen the beat of it. Knowed all the time that big possums climb little trees and little possums climb big trees, but I just be dogged if I ever heered tell of one that little running that far."

He studied the little possum carefully for a while, then finally glanced all around. "Why, if it ain't daybreak a'ready," he said in surprise. "Well, boys, I reckon we'll just have to call it a night and head in for home."

He'd turned to leave when I said: "You leaving this possum?"

"Why, he ain't big enough to skin," he said. "Just as well leave him."

Suddenly, it seemed to me that I just couldn't

107

stand to go home without something to show for our all-night hunt.

I went back and unwound the possum's tail from the tree branch and put him inside my coat pocket.

"I'll take him along and make a pet out of him," I said.

Restless nodded. "Good idea," he said. "Be a real curiosity, owning a possum that can run like a Mexican lion."

TEN

The .22 rifle that Jay got for not telling on Sis and Ruel was sure a dandy. As soon as he got it, Jay came for me, and we took to the woods to try it out.

We hunted in the direction of Grandpa Vesper's garden. As Jay pointed out, we might just as well collect a bounty on the cottontails we shot with his new gun as with the one that Grandpa furnished us.

But luck was against us. We hunted hard through Uncle Ike's pasture, through most of Uncle Wiley's, and all of Grandpa's, and the only shot we got was at a cottontail running like a house afire.

We missed him.

We arrived at the garden, tired and disgusted. We got us a drink. We pulled up some of Grandpa's carrots and ate them. We wasted some hulls, trying to hit a buzzard flying overhead, then went on up to the house to see if Grandma had dinner ready.

Luck was against us there, too. Grandma and Grandpa were gone, and all we could find in the kitchen was some cold cornbread. So we ate that and wandered out toward the lots.

And that's where we saw the big calf that Grandpa was fattening out to butcher.

The calf lay asleep in the sun. He lay almost between the shafts of an old two-wheeled cart that Grandpa used for hauling wood and hay. Lying back on the cart was the harness for the horse that pulled the cart.

Sight of the calf, the cart and the harness suggested the same thing to me and Jay, at the same time.

But Jay was the first to put it into words. "Bet we could get us a good ride in that cart if we hooked the calf to it."

I was a little disappointed that I hadn't made the suggestion first, but I didn't argue. I said I'd try it if he would, and Jay said he would, so we tried it.

We got a rope and dropped a loop over the calf's

head while he still lay on the ground. He was fat and lazy. He'd been an old milk calf, used to being roped away from a cow. He didn't fight a bit when we led him up to the snubbing post out in the middle of the pen.

We tied him up short. We wheeled the cart up behind him. We had to do some overhauling with the harness to make it fit, but we soon had the calf hooked up between the cart shafts. The only thing that wouldn't work was the bridle, and we got around this by making a sort of halter out of the bridle and snapping the reins into it.

I said, "I'll drive," but Jay said, "No, I'll drive. I thought of it first."

So we argued about that awhile. But Jay was older and bigger, so he got to drive. He said I could turn the calf loose from the snubbing post when he got ready. Then I could run open the lot gate and swing onto the back of the cart as he drove the calf through. That way, I could ride, too.

I untied the calf. I made a run for the lot gate and swung it open. But I didn't get to ride. Because the instant that the calf discovered that it was hooked to a cart, he wasn't a gentle calf any more. He reared straight up, walled his eyes, bellowed once, and came tearing through the gate so fast that my grab for the tail end of the cart missed, and I fell down in some fresh cow manure.

Jay didn't get much of a ride either. Once outside the pen, the calf went to pitching and bawling and kicking high at the cart. He circled wide and headed for a wire fence that stood alongside the road leading away from the house.

Jay did his best to turn the calf. He hauled back on the right rein until he had the slobbering runaway's head pulled clear around, facing him. But he still couldn't change the calf's direction of travel.

The calf hit the fence with a speed that had wires screeching through post staples for a hundred yards in both directions. He piled right on through, between the bottom and top wire.

The top wire was a barbed one. Jay saw it coming at him, at just the right level to saw his head off at the neck. He hollered "Whoa!" at the top of his voice and came rolling backward out of the cart. He hit the ground and bounced to his feet and hollered "Whoa!" louder than he had the first time.

But I guess the calf didn't hear him. He just dragged the cart through the fence and went off down the lane with it, still bawling and pitching and running.

And, of course, that's when old man Tate Ishum

had to come driving up the same lane in a wagon hooked to a span of spooky mules.

The mules took one look at what was heading toward them, snorted and quit the road so fast they nearly wrenched the tongue out of the wagon. They broke every wire in the fence as they went through it and took out down across a rocky, post-oak slant in a wild run. The wagon bounced from one boulder to the other. Old man Tate sawed the bits in the mules' mouths and hollered "Whoa!" with every breath.

The mules didn't pay any more attention to his "Whoas!" than the calf did to Jay's.

All this confusion added to the calf's scare, so that he quit the road and went through the opposite fence and headed off across a wide mesquite flat.

There was a deep, cut-banked gully in this flat. It was a narrow one, and the calf might have jumped it, if the cart hadn't been pulling back. Like it was, he jumped, and pitched head down into the gully, dragging the cart off the edge of the bank and down on top of him.

He was still lying in the bottom of the gulch, grunting and moaning a little, when Jay and I got there. The cart lay on top of him, holding him down. One of the cart's shafts was splintered, but not completely broken in two, and Jay figured it could be patched up all right with baling wire.

It wasn't much of a job to get the calf out from under the cart and lead him back to the pen. After his big scare, seemed like he was a gentle milk calf, like he'd always been. But what wore me and Jay down to a frazzle was hauling that cart out of the gully. We lifted and pushed and shoved and strained till it seemed like our eyeballs would pop out. And all the time, we just knew that Grandpa would come home and catch us at it.

But he didn't. We had the cart back in the pen and were both lying on the front gallery, deep in the sleep of exhaustion, when Grandma and Grandpa came driving up in a buckboard—with old man Tate Ishum standing behind them.

I never had liked old man Tate. He was the sort who would raise a row any time a kid swiped a melon out of his patch or a peach out of his orchard. And now, seeing him standing there, glaring at me and Jay and pointing an accusing finger at us, I liked him a lot less.

He was so angry that he could hardly talk; but from the best Jay and I could make out, we'd scared his mules till they'd not only run through four wire fences and cut themselves all to pieces, but they'd

115

overturned and wrecked a good wagon. On top of that, as old man Tate pointed out to Grandpa, anybody knew that once a span of young mules got a taste of running away, they were spoiled for good. You never could trust them again and you couldn't give them away to anybody who knew they'd ever run. Much less sell them for what they were worth.

Old man Tate declared that he wanted justice done and wanted it done in a hurry. And what he seemed to consider justice was to have Grandpa get out and give me and Jay the thrashing of our lives.

Grandpa Vesper sat there in the wagon, looking grave, till old man Tate ran down, then said: "Now, Mr. Ishum, if I was to give them boys a thrashing right here with you looking on, it might do them more harm than they've done your mules. And you wouldn't want that, now, would you?"

Old man Tate waved his fists in the air. "Want it," he shouted. "Of course, I want it. And I'm going to stand right here in this wagon till I see it done."

Grandpa got up out of his spring seat then and turned around and looked at old man Tate. He looked him square in the eye. "Now, Mr. Ishum," he said. "Them boys has got out of line. You'll git pay for your wagon and team, and I'll see that these boys is taken care of proper. But I can tell you one thing, Mr. Ishum. You can stand here in this wagon till the thing rots to pieces under you, and you still won't get to drool down these boys' necks while I whip 'em. Now you better go on back and take care of them runaway mules."

I don't know just how it happened. Grandpa Vesper wasn't nearly as big as old man Tate. But while the two of them stood there in the buckboard glaring at each other across the top of Grandma's head, it seemed like Grandpa went to growing in size, while old man Tate got smaller and smaller.

A second later, old man Tate turned and jumped out of the back of the buckboard and headed off down the road, almost in a trot.

I looked at Jay. He looked as relieved as I felt. We grinned a little, proud of the way Grandpa had run off old man Tate.

But a second later, we were worse scared than we'd been at first. That was when Grandma Elfie said to Grandpa in a begging voice: "You won't really be rough on the little fellers, will you, Vesper?"

"Rough on 'em," Grandpa said. "Why, Elfie, I'll make them little whistle britches recollect this for the rest of their lives!"

He got down out of the wagon. He left the team

to Grandma and headed toward the lots. "Come on, boys," he ordered.

We followed him, so scared we were sick. We watched him catch up and saddle a sorrel mare that was in the lot next to the one that held the calf. We waited till he'd mounted, then followed him through the gate and on down toward the creek.

"We'll search for the proper switches down there," he said.

He rode and we walked down to the creek. He searched through the brush. There was a thick stand of young china-ball sprouts growing close to the water. They were just about the size Papa generally cut when he took a notion to whip me. Grandpa spent a good long while examining these sprouts, but finally shook his head.

"I expect we could find better ones in Wiley's pasture," he said.

We followed his horse into Uncle Wiley's pasture. There were some china-ball sprouts growing there, too, but Grandpa rode right on past them and went to hunting through a patch of buckeye. He finally got out his knife and cut one. He trimmed it carefully from one end to the other. He held it up and gave it a trial whip through the air, and the swishing sound of it made my blood run cold.

The sound must have scared the sorrel mare, too, because she snorted and lunged aside and went to crowhop pitching with Grandpa. Which seemed to make Grandpa mad, so he worked the sorrel over so vigorously with the switch that he broke the end off it and had to throw it away.

"Never did like buckeye for a switch, nohow," he complained. "To tell the truth, walnut is about the only switch that's really worth anything when it comes to thrashing a boy."

He looked at me and Jay. "You boys know where there's any walnut growing?" he asked.

Jay looked at me. I'd been here longer and knew the country better.

I studied awhile. "Seems like," I said, "that I remember Restless Solomon's telling me about seeing some walnut growing along the creek on that old Felder place. But it's three or four miles down there."

Grandpa squinted at the sun. "I reckon we got time to make it before dark," he said. "But we'll have to hurry it up."

We hurried, all right. The sorrel had an easy saddle gait that didn't look like it was covering much ground till you tried to keep up afoot. Then you found that you had to stay in a trot all the time.

Jay and I trotted behind Grandpa's sorrel all the way to the old Felder place. By the time we got there, we were so tired we were ready to drop. And then we couldn't find any walnut. I was nearly certain that Restless had said there was some growing at this place, but I couldn't find it.

"Maybe it's further down the creek," Grandpa said and trotted us a piece further down the creek.

But there was none there, either. Grandpa looked worried.

"Well, I'll declare," he said. "I just don't hardly know what to do." He thought a minute, then added: "Unless we circle back by old man Tate Ishum's orchard and cut some peach sprouts. Peach ain't bad, but walnut's better."

When I thought how far it was to old man Tate's peach orchard, I wanted to cry. Jay and I had nearly killed ourselves getting that cart out of that gully. Then we'd had this long fast trot, with the dread of what was coming sapping our strength. I just didn't see how I could possibly make it all the way over to old man Tate's peach orchard.

I said nervously: "Old man Tate never did like for us to get in his peach orchard."

Grandpa grinned. "I bet this is one time we could go in there without his raising a squawk."

I looked at Jay. I guess he was feeling as bad as I was because I could see a hint of tears in his eyes.

"Grandpa," I begged, "couldn't we just use a mesquite or something?"

"With thorns?" he said in surprise.

Jay's lips went to quivering. "Well, you could trim the thorns off a little, couldn't you?"

Grandpa sat on his sorrel and considered. "Well," he conceded, "I guess we could. If you boys'll locate the right kind. But I don't want you picking out no little old switches. I want 'em big enough to count."

So to keep from having to dog-trot all the way to old man Tate's peach orchard, Jay and I got out and went to searching hard for the right kind of a sprout to get a whipping with.

We found a lot of them that looked good enough to us, but Grandpa wouldn't have them. They were too crooked or too thorny or too limber or too small. Mostly they were too small.

When I pointed out a hackberry that I thought was plenty big, he gave me a look like he must have given old man Tate Ishum back there in the wagon. Anyhow, it was the sort of look that sent me running, tired as I was, in search of something bigger.

"Now, I'll tell you boys," Grandpa warned sternly. "You just as well quit wasting your time, showing me them little bitty switches. What I want and what I aim to have is one heavy enough to make you get high behind every lick."

We were desperate. We ran this way and looked that till our leg muscles were jerking and trembling, and still Grandpa kept us going.

It was nearly dark and we'd hunted down into a bottom along Recollection Creek before Jay pointed fearfully to a couple of young cottonwoods. "Are these big enough, Grandpa?" he asked.

When I saw the size of them, I was appalled. They were ten feet long, at least, with bottoms thicker than the butts of buggy whips. If Grandpa chose them and swung them hard at all, he'd cut us in two.

But by then, I was so worn out and full of dread that it didn't seem to matter much. Just any sort of whipping would do, if only Grandpa would get it over with.

Grandpa studied the switches a good long while before he nodded. "Well, they ain't much," he said, "but it's getting late. I reckon they'll have to do."

He got down and cut the switches. He did a careful job of trimming them. Then he lifted one and cut the air with it, and the whistle it made ran cold chills all through me.

"Well, bow your backs," he said to me and Jay.

We went to blubbering then. We turned our backs, waiting submissively for the first blows to fall.

Instead, Grandpa burst out laughing. He came and hugged us both up tight.

"Now, boys," he said, "I'll tell you. I've cut some mighty fine switches which I'm going to leave here on the creek bank. And my advice is the next time you get the itch to get into some devilment, you come down here and use these switches for fishing instead."

Then he laughed some more and went and got on his horse and rode off, leaving us to come home whenever we felt able.

Grandpa sure told the truth about one thing: we never forgot that punishment for the rest of our lives.

ELEVEN

It was a good long while before Grandpa Vesper made his second try for the graveyard gobbler. He wanted to give that old bird plenty of time to get over his first scare.

Then one foggy morning, he got up real early and saddled his horse. He rode out while the coyotes were still singing for daylight and was holed up in a tight nest of bamboo briars surrounding my Great-uncle Monk Scallon's grave when the east began to gray behind the timber.

This blind didn't suit Grandpa as well as his fa-

vorite one behind Great-grandpa Mill-Wheel's head-
stone; it was a little too far from the opening he
hoped to call the gobbler into and didn't give him
quite as wide a sight range. But it was farther from
the granite ledge. Grandpa didn't figure the bobcat
ever grew that could jump from the ledge to Uncle
Monk's grave.

He squatted down on his hunkers, listening. He
listened for a long time and heard nothing. Then,
finally, his ears picked up the cautious movements
of some animal off to the left and a good long ways
behind him. He listened hard and decided it was a
range hog nosing through the leaf beds after acorns.
A lot of range hogs in those days could move about
in the woods quieter than any deer. You never heard
one grunt.

Soon after that, Grandpa heard a single turkey
fly down from a roost a couple or three hundred
yards up the creek. He heard the sound that the big
clumsy wings made pounding the air. He heard the
rattle of some brush as the turkey landed. He heard
some sleepy birds twitter, and then there was complete silence again.

Daylight came, and a slight breeze set in motion
the wreaths of heavy fog hanging in the basin.
Grandpa was satisfied. If he'd heard several turkeys

leave their roosts, he wouldn't have had a chance. The gobbler he wanted wouldn't be roosting where turkeys hung out in bunches. But that one turkey he'd heard—his wings had sounded mighty heavy. Grandpa guessed that this was his old graveyard gobbler, all right.

He laid his gun across a fence rail and lifted his turkey-bone caller.

The first soft note got an immediate answer. But it was from the wrong direction. And the sound of it puzzled Grandpa. It came from the left and behind him and the notes were a little too soft for a gobbler, yet mighty coarse, too, for a hen turkey. He waited a long time; the answer he'd gotten wasn't from the gobbler he wanted.

When finally Grandpa ventured to call again, he got the right answer from the right direction. It came from up the creek, and Grandpa would have recognized that hoarse, wary yelp anywhere. It was his lone graveyard gobbler, and the old hermit was talking to him.

Then from behind Grandpa came that curious yelp he'd heard the first time. Only it was closer now, less than a hundred yards away, the best he could calculate.

Grandpa Vesper frowned and peered behind him

through the last wisps of fog that hovered over the graveyard and seemed reluctant to fade. A second turkey that close was almost sure to ruin his chances with the big one.

Grandpa studied the situation. He wondered if he could maybe frighten this second turkey away without scaring him into sounding the alarm signal that would put the big gobbler on guard. The odds were long, but that looked like Grandpa's only chance. Carefully, he shifted his feet under him and brushed the briars with one hand, making a slight rustling sound.

A shotgun roared in the fog. A withering blast of No. 4 shot tore through the briars. Three of them caught Grandpa Vesper in the rear, driving deep and burning like red-hot spikes.

Grandpa leaped to his feet with a howl. He dropped his gun. He jumped two graves, stumbled on the footstone of a third, and sprawled belly down across the fourth. He lay there in the dead weeds, wallowing and pitching and hollering.

Grandpa got himself in hand in time to catch sight of a man streaking through the brush, clutching a double-barreled shotgun in one hand. The man was running like the devil was on his tail. The fog was too thick for Grandpa to make out who it was; but if he could have got his hands on his Winchester in time, he would have got a real close-up look. Like it was, he ran back and grabbed up his rifle and emptied the magazine in the general direction of the running man, then stood and waved his fists and yelled at him as long as he thought the second hunter was in hearing distance.

Grandma Elfie didn't ask her man one question when he came crippling back to the house, leading a horse he wasn't able to straddle. She just hunted up her tweezers and spaying needle, like Grandpa ordered, and went to digging for the buried shot.

She put Grandpa across the kitchen table, with his legs hanging off one side and his head and arms off the other. She told me and Jay to hang on to his legs and arms with all our weight and try to hold him down while she worked.

Like I say, Grandma didn't quarrel at Grandpa for going back to turkey-hunt in the old Scallon graveyard. But it seemed to me that she wasn't nearly as gentle as she might have been as she probed deep for those shot.

Grandpa grunted and groaned and twisted and squirmed till it was all Jay and I could do to hold him down. If he hadn't been such a little old dried-up man, we never could have done it, either.

129

Grandpa swore that he'd get the man who'd shot him if it was the last thing he ever did on earth. He said he'd go back there and trail him, if he had to crawl on his hands and knees and smell out the scent like a hound. He said Texas wasn't big enough to hold him and the man who'd call turkeys with a green leaf, then shoot them with a shotgun. He said any man who'd call turkeys that way was exactly the kind of belly-crawling sneak to cut down a man with a shotgun, then high-tail it out of gun range when he saw it wasn't a turkey he'd shot.

I don't know just how Grandpa came by the notion that the man who shot him had been calling with a green leaf, but he was convinced that it was so. The spaying needle gouging into his seat was sure hurting, and I guess Grandpa had to take the hurt out on somebody. I'm pretty sure that right there, with me and Jay doing all we could to hold him across that table, Grandpa Vesper got as mad as Uncle Ike ever got.

He kept on talking and raving like that till we'd learned the whole story and Grandma had finally removed the shot. Then Grandma helped him to bed and called me and Jay out into the yard, away from the house.

"Now, you boys skin out for Restless Solomon's house and tell him I said to keep scarce for a while."

I looked at Grandma in astonishment. "You mean it was Restless? How do you know?"

"Quiet!" Grandma Elfie warned me. "I don't, not for sure. And I don't care. All I know is that I happened to overhear that poor little old woman of his claim that he calls with a green leaf. And if your grandpa ever finds that out, there'll be a killing, whether it was Restless or not. And we don't want a killing."

Jay and I went to warn Restless, but we got there too late. His woman said he'd just left the house. She said he'd learned of a wood-cutting job over in the next county and she expected him to be gone for a couple or three weeks.

There was a scared look in her eyes when she told us this; and I noticed that while she talked, she went to a lot of trouble to stand between us and a double-barreled shotgun lying across the bed behind her.

TWELVE

We were at Gritville, two miles down the creek from Squaw Springs where Uncle Adam Creech had his grist mill. Jay and I had gone over there to visit our cousin Lode. Lode was Uncle Gabriel and Aunt Judy Creech's boy. Uncle Gabriel ran the Gritville *Herald*, a weekly newspaper better known as *Gabriel's Horn*.

I was mighty proud of my cousin Lode. He could do the best job of crossing his eyes and waggling his ears, at the same time, of anybody I ever saw. But I didn't get to visit him often. This was because Lode was a "town boy," and most mamas along Recollection Creek were convinced that town boys were wild and would get a body into trouble.

As it turned out, they were right. Lode sure got me and Jay into a mess of trouble.

Jay and I were out back of Uncle Gabriel's office feeding clabber milk to Aunt Judy's baby turkeys when Lode came bursting through the back door. In one hand, he gripped a paper-wrapped side of bacon that Aunt Judy had sent him to the store for. He was panting hard from running with such a load, and his eyes were wide with excitement.

He saw me and Jay, but didn't stop till he'd run up close to the house and flung his bacon through an open window onto the kitchen table. Then he came tearing back, calling for us to follow.

Jay and I couldn't figure out what all the excitement was about, but we could see that it was too big to waste time on questions, so we followed.

We ran through the news office and out onto the sidewalk. There we saw a kid by the name of Crawfish Turner running toward us with his shirttail flopping. Crawfish was as bug-eyed as Lode. His freckles stood out on his face like spent bird shot sticking to a whitewashed wall.

Crawfish tried to talk, but had to stop first and swallow. So Lode was the first to say it.

"Fruit!" he gasped. "Apples, bananas, oranges, grapes!"

"A whole wagonload!" Crawfish added.

I stood and stared at Crawfish and Lode. I didn't believe it. Nobody ever saw a whole wagonload of fruit like that. Not here at the tail end of winter, anyhow.

You've got to understand that in those days a kid didn't pester his daddy for a nickel and run down to the corner grocery for an apple or an orange. In the first place, nickels were scarce and hard to come by, so nobody threw them around. In the second place, even the big general merchandise stores that carried everything from steel plow points to long-handled drawers still didn't stock perishables. At Christmas, somebody might risk bringing in enough apples and oranges to fill a few stockings and help decorate the church trees. But from then on, what fresh fruit a kid got, he rustled for himself. In season, he could pay visits of a night to near-by plum thickets and peach orchards. Out of season, he did without.

So you can see why I was so dumbfounded at the idea of anybody's showing up in town at this time of the year with a whole wagonload of rare fruits.

But, sure enough, when we all tore around the

corner, there stood a wagonload of fruit in front of the hotel, with old Mrs. Hobbs picking around over it, pinching and squeezing things to see if they were soft ripe. Like maybe she was used to buying fine fruit every day.

We ran up close and stood with our mouths watering. I said to Jay: "You got any of that money you been getting from Sis and Ruel?"

Jay suddenly looked haggard and sick. "I spent it all," he admitted. "I spent it all last week for licorice!"

Crawfish and Lode stared at Jay accusingly. Jay's face got hot. "Well, it was my money!" he defended.

Mrs. Hobbs selected about enough fruit to feed a sick bird, then started beating the peddler down on the price.

The peddler was a sad-eyed little Mexican with a droopy hat, droopy mustaches, and a droopy slump to his shoulders. He looked like he'd spent a lot of his life trying to stand up against sharp-bargaining women like old Mrs. Hobbs and hadn't had much luck at it. He argued, but you could tell he didn't expect to win. Finally, he took a third less than his asking price and drove on down the street, looking more droopy than ever.

We followed; we couldn't help it. We kept our

distance, but we followed, just to feast our eyes on all that fruit.

It was the bananas that nearly drove me crazy. Big old bunches of yellow-hided bananas, with little spots of black beginning to show. Just right for eating.

The peddler pulled up next in front of Mrs. Rank's house and rattled a little bell. Mrs. Rank came out and saw what he had and said "Oh, goody!" just like a kid of a girl might have done. And she bought a whole bunch of bananas!

That nearly took my breath.

I guessed Mrs. Rank could buy bananas by the bunch, all right, what with the stacks of money her man piled up over there in the town bank. Womenfolks claimed she was a spendthrift, and it was even whispered about that one time she made a trip all the way to San Antonio to get herself a fancy hairdo. Only Mama never would believe that one.

"She's young and flighty," Mama admitted, "but even a banker's wife wouldn't throw away good money on any such tomfoolery!"

Right now, though, I wasn't so sure. Anybody who'd buy a whole bunch of bananas was bound to be a mighty reckless spender.

Before the peddler left Mrs. Rank's house, here

came Tom McDougal's wife and Miss Nervy Allison. They saw the fruit on Mrs. Rank's gallery, and I heard Mrs. McDougal speak up sharp and loud: "Well, we're not banking people, but if *her* man can buy a whole bunch, my Tom can do the same." So she and Miss Nervy packed off a whole bunch between them.

Around the corner, the peddler sold half a bunch to Lin Moore's wife, along with some oranges. And two big sacks full of bananas to that flirty Naylor girl.

It hurt me, the way those women made such a big hole so fast in that banana pile. Any minute now, they'd all be gone, and we wouldn't get any.

Lode got panicky and tore out home to see if he could raise any money. But we knew better. Owners of country newspapers never had any money. They swapped too many subscriptions for sweet potatoes, hog lard, and homemade molasses. After five years, Uncle Gabriel was still saving for a new press.

It didn't even enter Crawfish's head to run home for money. Crawfish's mama was a widow woman who took in washing. All he could do was follow along with me and Jay, helping us feel sorry for ourselves.

Even Dev Anders's two little old twisty girls

showed up with a dime for apples, and Crawfish said it was common knowledge that Dev Anders owed everybody in town.

Lode came back with his shirttail hanging limp and wearing a hopeless look on his face. He didn't have to tell us that he'd failed.

Our last little hope was gone now—and our appetites were desperate.

That's all the excuse I've got for what we did when the peddler finally pulled up his rig in the shade of a big mesquite back of Heinemeier's store, fixing to noon.

He unhooked his horse and led it off to water. And there sat that big load of fruit—completely unprotected.

Even then, I don't think we would have stolen it, big as the temptation was. I really think it was John Jenkins and Bert Hawkins who drove us to it.

Bert and John came out of the alley back of the hotel, pulling a little red wagon full of junk brass they'd picked up to sell. John was runty and redheaded and the preacher's son, and Bert was nearly as tall and gangly as his daddy, Sheriff Dave Hawkins. John and Bert had pretty bad reputations. That was because they had to go to so much extra trouble to show folks they could be as tough as other boys, in spite of their daddies being such drawbacks. They looked up and saw us being tempted, and John said "Lord!" in a praying sort of voice, and Bert whistled real low. He gave a quick glance all around, then barked at us: "Well, what are you waiting for? It'll be too late when he gets back!" And he dropped his wagon handle and ran toward the peddler's rig.

That was all that was needed to stampede the rest of us.

In two jumps, we were up on the wagon and back off, then streaking down the alley. Bert and I lugged a big banana stalk between us. The others led the way, loaded with grapes and oranges and apples.

At the end of the alley, we dived under the barb-wire fence, rolled to our feet, and tore out down through the bee-myrtle thickets in Banker Rank's cow pasture, running faster than ever. We never slacked till we went in under the low-hanging grapevines on the bank of a little running creek. This was where the town boys had themselves a private hide-out.

There we had us a feast. It was the best feast I ever ate.

This beat anything we'd ever done. We all agreed on that. It was way better than snitching water-melons.

We sat there in the shade of the grapevines, stuffing ourselves and bragging about our boldness.

Inside me, though, I had an uneasy feeling. I kept recollecting the droopy little peddler and how old Mrs. Hobbs had beaten him down on price. I didn't much like snitching from somebody like that. I'd rather have snitched from old Mrs. Hobbs. Also, there was the prospect of burning for eternity in hell's fire and brimstone. I'd heard John Jenkins's daddy at a brush-arbor meeting one time tell how it felt to burn for eternity in hell's fire and brimstone, and after that, every time I snitched something, I couldn't help recollecting.

But I didn't let on that I was worried. I laughed and bragged with the rest, and finally got into an eating contest with Bert.

I ate sixteen bananas to his fourteen.

Nobody ate less than a dozen. We were full up to our ears when we finally swung our banana stalk, still half full, to an overhanging tree branch. We sneaked back to town then, each by a different route so nobody seeing us come out of the brush would suspect.

Aunt Judy had fried chicken for dinner and threatened me and Jay and Lode with castor oil when she saw we weren't much hungry. So, to dodge the oil, we ate as much as we could, but it was sure rough going, stuffing that chicken down on top of all those bananas.

After dinner, Aunt Judy sent us to Heinemeier's store for a spool of thread. While the clerk hunted for the right color, we looked out back. There we saw the peddler and Sheriff Hawkins standing beside the wagon. The peddler had his hat off and was talking fast, mostly with his hands. When he pointed up the alley and then at his load of fruit, it was plenty plain what he was talking about.

The sheriff looked sober. He walked over and pulled John and Bert's junk wagon up beside the peddler's rig. He lifted his hat and scratched his head.

And that's when old man Tate came hurrying up. He went straight to Sheriff Hawkins. We couldn't hear what he was saying, but we could see that he was talking fast and convincingly. A minute later, he was leading Sheriff Hawkins off down the alley, pointing to the ground as he went. And where we'd gone through the wire fence close to Mrs. Rank's house, he reached down and picked up a fallen banana. He shook it in the sheriff's face.

I looked at Jay, then looked away.

After Grandpa Vesper had trotted us all over the

country that day hunting switches, Jay and I had felt paid up for scaring old man Tate's mules into a runaway. So we'd promptly forgotten all about it. But the old man evidently hadn't. That cranky old devil had been laying for us. And now he was blabbing everything he knew to Sheriff Hawkins.

Aunt Judy looked at me over her spectacles when we came back with the thread. "Hopper," she said with concern, "are you feeling all right?"

"Yessum," I lied, "I'm feeling just fine."

"Well, you look mighty peaked and bilious to me. I still think I ought to give you a good dose of castor oil."

Uncle Gabriel stepped through the door just in time to save me.

"No, you won't give that boy castor oil," he stormed. "Now, Judy, you listen to me. I had enough of that stuff poured down me when I was a boy to purge all my descendants for the next three generations. I don't see what gets into womenfolks, anyhow. Never happy without chasing some poor little old defenseless kid around with a tablespoon full of castor oil. Be darned if I don't believe I'll go write an editorial about it!"

That made Aunt Judy mad, of course, and she started arguing with Uncle Gabriel. But Uncle Gabriel got mad, too, and argued louder. It all wound up with Aunt Judy in tears and Uncle Gabriel's stamping out to the office to set a hot editorial with a heading of "Women and the Castor Oil Craze."

So I escaped the castor oil; but none of us escaped Sheriff Hawkins. He stepped into the office a few minutes later with a look in his eyes that turned my blood cold.

Just before he showed up, I'd about convinced myself that we were safe. I didn't see how any man, even a bloodhound lawman like Sheriff Hawkins, could bring himself to arrest and jail his own flesh and blood. But I could see now that I was wrong. Because just outside the door behind the sheriff stood his boy Bert, looking as white in the face as a bed sheet. And beside Bert was John, trying to swallow something he couldn't get down.

Behind them all stood old man Tate Ishum, with his eyes as sharp and eager as a fox's, grinning and licking his lips. Like he was tasting something mighty good.

Sheriff Hawkins said to Uncle Gabriel: "Gabriel, if you can spare these here boys for a while, I'd like to take them along on a little party I've rigged up for some up-and-coming citizens."

Any other time Uncle Gabriel would have wanted

to know what it was all about. But right now he was so deep in his castor-oil editorial that he hardly looked up.

"Sure, Dave," he said over his shoulder. "Take them right along."

I knew then the awful despair a man feels when the hangman comes for him.

I wondered what Papa would do when he learned that his son was a thief and a jailbird. I thought of Mama; a blow like this would break her. Likely, when she came to talk to me through the cold prison bars, her hair would be snow white. She'd read me a story one time about a mother's hair turning snow white overnight when her boy went to prison.

I figured Sheriff Hawkins would pull his pearl-handled gun and march us up the street ahead of it. Instead he led the way, with us all following. Seemed like it hadn't entered his head that, as desperate as we were, we might make a break for it.

I thought of making a break, and I guess the others did. And I guess the reason they didn't was the same one that held me. We'd all been in town the day that Sheriff Hawkins brought back that jail-breaking horse thief, tied hands-to-feet under the belly of a horse, and with his vacant eyes staring at the ground.

As deadly as we knew Sheriff Hawkins to be with that six-shooter, we all felt, I guess, that we just couldn't afford to take a chance.

Instead of taking us to jail, Sheriff Hawkins led straight up the alley, past the Rank house. Old man Tate followed along behind, grinning maliciously at me and Jay, till we got to the place where we'd all gone through the wire fence. Then Sheriff Hawkins noticed him and said: "Mr. Ishum, I guess we can get along all right without you."

Old man Tate looked crushed. He tried to argue. "But, Sheriff, I was the one what showed you—"

"Yeah, I know," Sheriff Hawkins broke in. "You've done a great service for society, Mr. Ishum, and we all appreciate it. But now that your duty's done, the law'll take over."

Old man Tate stood watching us climb through the fence. He looked like he'd been robbed of something that was rightfully his.

The dirty, sneaking old devil! I made myself a promise right there that someday I'd break out of prison and come back for him. He'd pay for this!

The town boys had always claimed that their hide-out was so secret nobody could find it. But Sheriff Hawkins led us as straight to it as a bee can go to water. There, under the grapevines, he reached up and lifted down our half-full banana stalk.

"Now, boys," he said. "Mrs. Rank thought enough of you little devils to pay for what you stole. And just to show you that I think a heap of you, too, I'm going to set right here and watch while you eat up everything she paid for. *Now get to eating!*"

The way he said it, looking at us with those hard eyes, nobody argued. We ate. We ate till we were pop-eyed. We ate till it seemed as if bananas and apples and grapes could start running out of our ears. And still he kept us at it.

Along toward the last, his boy Bert tried to balk on him. But when the sheriff started unbuckling his cowhide belt, Bert's appetite picked up again.

We ate till the last little shriveled-up banana was gone.

Then the sheriff gave us each a separate fierce look and headed back for town without saying another word.

We didn't say anything either. We were too stuffed and too stunned. We just sat around, looking at each other, then looking away, till finally, being mighty careful about it, we got to our feet and silently left the shade.

When Jay and Lode and I staggered into Aunt

Judy's house, we were swelled up like poisoned pups. We tried to sneak off and go to bed, but Aunt Judy heard us.

She came hurrying to the door with a paper sack clutched in her hands and a guilty look on her face.

"Boys," she said, "Gabriel made me so mad this morning about the castor oil that I just up and spent some of his press money. I'm ashamed about it now, but what's done is done; and if you all will eat up this fruit before he comes back to the house, maybe he won't ever know about it."

We were clear across the room from Aunt Judy, but I was smelling those bananas before she ever finished talking.

I wheeled and headed for the back door. I just barely made it in time. So did Lode. But Jay didn't. Jay got it all over Aunt Judy's floor.

THIRTEEN

In spite of his bad back and the dire predictions of his neighbors, Restless Solomon managed to get in a crop that spring. He got his planting done earlier than most, too, and the rains fell right and it all came up and looked so good that Uncle Ike was impressed.

"By golly!" he said to Papa one day when he drove past in his wagon. "Do you reckon that shiftless thing really aims to settle down and make a crop?"

"Why, you know better than that," Papa said. "Wait till the sun gets hot."

But it wasn't the hot sun that kept Restless from making a crop that year. It was a piece he read in Uncle Gabriel's paper.

I remember it like yesterday, the day Restless read that piece. Jay and I had been off squirrel hunting and had wound up at Restless's place at dinnertime. We'd skinned our squirrels and turned them over to Restless's woman to fry for dinner and were sitting out on the front gallery, resting and waiting to eat. And Restless was sitting there with his shoes off, looking through the paper, when suddenly he jumped up out of his chair and stood with both fists clenched.

"It's a cinch!" he exclaimed. "Boys, I tell you, it's a double-dyed, lead-pipe cinch!"

We stared up at him in wonder. It was plain to see that Restless had just been struck by a mighty powerful idea of some kind.

"What's a cinch?" Jay wanted to know.

Restless flung up his hand and held it, cocking one ear toward the outdoors. "Listen," he said. "What do you hear?"

We sat up and listened.

Jay said: "Why, all I hear is them squirrels fry-ing."

"No," Restless said impatiently. "Further away from the house. What do you hear?"

"You mean that old rooster quail that's whis-tling?" I asked.

"That's it!" Restless exclaimed, bringing his up-raised hand down with an air-cutting stroke. "Quail! Bobwhite quail. Right here on this farm, I've got the best natural quail-raising grounds there is in the whole United States. Read that!"

He shoved the crumpled paper at me and Jay. We took it and started reading the piece he pointed to with his finger. The piece told about how some man back east was raising bobwhite quail in captivity and selling them at a big profit to people who'd killed off all their quail and wanted to restock their places. It said that from a start of forty pairs, the man had raised sixteen hundred young quail, which brought him a dollar and a half a head when grown.

Before Jay and I could finish reading, Restless started pacing the floor and making plans and count-ing the profits.

"You boys could help me," he said. "We could start with fifty pair. Maybe more. Just owing to how many quail eggs we can locate and hatch off . . . Say we start with a hundred pair. That's fifty hens. Let them lay thirty eggs apiece and raise the young. That's fifteen hundred right there. From them we raise . . . let's see now . . . that's seven hundred and fifty times thirty eggs. That'd be twenty-two thousand and five hundred. And half of them laying thirty eggs apiece. . . . Why, goshamighty, dang. Wouldn't be no time till we'd run it to a million. And at a dollar and a half a head . . . !"

Restless stopped pacing the floor and went to shaking his head like maybe the flies were after him.

I had the same feeling. This was getting rich the quickest I'd ever heard tell about!

Well, you can see how Restless came to neglect his crop that spring. As he pointed out to his woman while we ate fried squirrel and made our plans, "It'd be a mighty short-sighted fool who'd piddle off his time with a little old two-bit crop when he had a cool million dollars looking him right in the face."

Restless's woman was a sort of faded-out, mousy-looking little person who always seemed too tired to talk. She didn't talk now. She just stared at Restless a minute, holding a squirrel leg between her teeth, then finally went back to chewing on it.

Quail nests turned out to be harder to find than

we'd counted on. The woods were full of bobwhites; we could hear them whistling and calling to each other all over the place. But it took us better than two weeks of hard searching to locate three nests.

However, one of these nests held more eggs than we thought a quail ever laid. One had fifteen, one twenty-two, and one thirty-six. That was seventy-three eggs in all. Not quite a hundred, but a mighty good start.

Restless seemed satisfied. "Maybe we don't find any more," he said. "Don't matter. There's enough here to make us all dirt rich."

We took the eggs and set them under an old brown leghorn hen that Restless's woman had. The hen was setting on a pile of shucks in one corner of a little shed room of his house that he used for a corncrib.

The hen took the eggs without any fuss, even seemed glad to get them, the way she reached out and started raking them under her feathers with her beak. But then, three weeks later, when the eggs hatched, she went crazy.

We never did know exactly what happened, of course. Restless just got woke up one morning by a big commotion in the shed room. He jumped up out of bed and grabbed his shotgun, thinking it was a varmint after our quail eggs. But when he peered through the cracks, the only thing he could see was little baby quail, about the size of big bumblebees, swarming all over the shed room. And running back and forth through them was the leghorn hen, squawking and flapping her wings like she was scared clear out of her wits.

Restless ran around to the outside door and flung it open, still looking for the varmint that had scared the hen. But that proved a mistake. Evidently the hen had been looking for a way to get out. She rose from the floor with a squawk and flew straight at Restless's head. He ducked, and she went past. The last he ever saw of her, she was streaking it off toward the creek, still squawking and cackling.

"The only thing I could ever figure out," Restless said, "is that the dang fool just couldn't believe the sight of what she'd hatched off."

Whatever it was, she'd left us in a pickle. All those baby quail on our hands, with no hen to mother them.

"We'll have to stir around and try to borrow another setting hen," Restless said. "And do it in a hurry. Before all them little biddies scatter out and get away."

It was early in the year for chicken hens to be

setting, but we still figured that somebody along Recollection Creek would have one. But they didn't. We tried all the Creeches and the Savages and then everybody else we could think of. And not a one had a setting hen. Then we thought of Aaron Blood, and went to see him, but he didn't have one, either.

But he did have an idea. "Why don't you try old man Tate Ishum?" he said. "I hear tell he's got a hen that'll play mama to just about anything. Feller tells me she'll raise ducks, guineas, and geese, all in the same bunch. Claims it's a fact she one time raised three kittens!"

Well, of course Jay and I knew that we couldn't borrow a chicken hen or anything else from old man Tate. We explained why to Restless and Aaron Blood. And Restless was afraid that maybe he couldn't, either, on account of the time he and old man Tate had had a little difference over the matter of who owned a pecan tree that Restless had threshed. So Aaron Blood offered to go along and pretend that he was the one wanting to borrow the hen. Only that didn't work, either, because by the time we got to old man Tate's house, the word had already gotten around about the big money-making quail business we were in. And, of course, anybody as greedy and vindictive as old man Tate Ishum wasn't going to miss a chance to make us pay for anything we got.

"Oh, I'll let you have the hen," he said. "But she'll cost you."

"How much?" Restless said.

"Why, I reckon I'd have to have half interest in them quail," he said.

Restless jumped straight up. "Half interest!" he shouted in alarm. "Why, dangamighty, this is a million-dollar business. You expect me to give away half a million dollars for the use of a setting hen?"

"Why, no," old man Tate said, "not if you ain't a mind to. I've got that old hen on a setting of eggs right now, and we can just leave her there."

It was high-handed robbery, of course, but what could we do? It was that or nothing. We took the hen.

She was a big old fussy game hen that nearly pecked Restless's hands off before we got her home. But she was a good one. The minute we put her inside the shed room, she started clucking, calling the little baby quail out of their hiding places among the corn-shuck litter. And by the way she turned her feathers all wrong-side-out and tried to fight any of us who stepped inside the shed, we knew that she'd protect her brood. She'd cost us heavy, but it was plain that she had our interests at heart.

Of course, we were all pretty bitter about how old man Tate had robbed us; but as Restless pointed out: "Half a million is a pretty sizable chunk of money." So Jay and I went home that night still convinced that great wealth was right at our finger tips.

FOURTEEN

In those days, I spent a good bit of time dreaming about going off somewhere and digging me up a buried treasure and being independent rich for the rest of my life.

But it wasn't a treasure I was after the day I found that one was buried in the china-ball grove back of Bald Knob. All I had in mind that morning was to get away from the house before Papa came in from the pasture.

When Mama got a chance to tell Papa what I'd done to her old dominecker rooster, I didn't want to be anywhere around.

I went over the catclaw ridge back of the barn at a hard run. I had to slow down some for the old laid-out field just beyond; it was overgrown with tall grass burs, and the only way a barefooted boy could cross was to jump from one gopher mound to the next. But from there on, it was clear sailing through the post-oak woods to Bald Knob.

The big china-ball grove stood on a slant just the other side of the Knob. I crossed an opening and entered the shade of the trees. I trotted the length of the long black boulder that walled one side. I rounded the end of the rock and stopped dead in my tracks.

There was a man in the grove!

I'd been there dozens of times before, and there'd never been anybody there. But there was a man there now. He sat in an awkward body-twisting position beneath the lip of the boulder and held a cocked six-shooter pointed straight at me!

It wasn't the gun so much that scared me. It was the wild, trapped-animal look on the man's face, the bitter curl of his sun-cracked lips, the fierce hard shine in his puckered gray eyes.

Almost instantly, the man's eyes widened and the hardness went out of his face, leaving it slack and gray under the dark stubble of his beard. He low-

ered the gun to his lap. He leaned against a sapling.

"Howdy, boy," he said.

I stood rooted to the ground.

The man was dressed in black cowhand clothes, with bench-made boots and a new black hat. On a cartridge-studded belt was a cutaway scabbard for the gun he held in his lap. His eyes looked tired— tired and somehow sick. His eyes moved all over me, slowly, giving me the feeling that he was making a close study of something he hadn't seen in a long time.

"You come here often?" he asked.

"Pretty often," I said, then blurted out nervously, "mostly, just when I get into trouble back at the house."

He smiled faintly. "You in trouble now?"

"Pretty bad," I said. "If Mama's old dominecker rooster dies, Papa'll sure lay it on me."

A real smile came then, warm and friendly. I felt the fear drain out of me.

The man didn't ask what I'd done to Mama's old dominecker rooster, but suddenly I was all eagerness to explain.

"I guess maybe I've killed him with a grain of corn," I said. "I kept feeding it to him and then jerking it back out."

"Jerking it back out?" The man frowned, not understanding.

"Sure," I said. "I had the grain of corn tied onto a string. I'd let him pick it up and swallow it down, then jerk it back up his long neck. It sure made that old rooster squawk and flop around, but he'd always pick it up and swallow it again. . . . Then Mama, she caught me at it."

The man tipped back his head, as if he were about to let loose with a big laugh. But all that came out was a grunting sort of chuckle that seemed to pain him somewhere inside. His face sobered; his tired eyes searched me closer.

"How come you pulling a dirty trick like that on your mama's rooster?" he demanded.

"Because the rascal's mean," I told him. "This morning he ran right up and flogged me and then bit me."

I unbuckled a suspender strap and pulled down the bib of my overalls. I showed the man where the rooster had pecked my navel and made the blood come.

He studied my wound and nodded his sympathy. "Served the old devil right to have that corn dragged out of him," he said gravely.

He kept sitting there in that peculiar twisted position and began staring up at the white blooms of the china-ball trees.

"This is a good place to come when you're in trouble," he said after a while. "I used to come here regular."

I stared at him. I wondered who he was and how he'd got here. I couldn't see any horse around.

"You used to live hereabouts some place?" I inquired.

"Just around the point of the Knob. I was just about big enough to fill them overalls of yours then."

I recollected then the old house place there. Once there'd been a fire-blackened chimney standing out from a couple of live oaks, a lonesome-looking thing, without a house to go with it. Then somebody had hauled the rocks away—to build another chimney with, I guess.

I'd wondered some about the folks who had once lived in that house and if they had a boy who liked slipping off to secret places, like the grove. And now here was the boy.

But, somehow, I couldn't see the big lean hard man in front of me getting into a jam with his mama and running off from the house. I just couldn't see it at all.

I said: "You in bad trouble now?"

164

"Pretty bad," he said.

I waited for him to tell about it, but he didn't. All he did was sit there and stare up at the china-ball blooms with the wild bees humming around them. His eyes were nearly shut.

After a while, I said, "Is that how come you came back to the grove?"

"Yes," he said. "It started me to recollecting something here that I'd left behind. Something I had to see one more time."

I looked all around the grove. Then I noticed, just the other side of the sapling he leaned against, an uptilted slab of rock. There was a hole there, with the open lid of a metal box sticking out.

I felt my heart jump. "A treasure!" I gasped.

The man's eyes met mine.

"That's it, boy," he said with conviction. "A real treasure that I buried too many years ago. The finest a man can ever store up."

The thought struck me then how many times I'd lain right in these leaves and dreamed about digging up a buried treasure. And all that time I'd been this close to one!

Back up the slant of Bald Knob, a loose rock clinked against another; there was the rattle of brush dragging against saddle leather.

165

The man gave a convulsive heave and flopped over on his stomach. He clawed for the lid of the metal box, slamming it shut. He jerked the flat slab down on top of it. One broad swipe of his hand raked dry leaves over the place, hiding it.

"Now, let 'em come," he said in a harsh voice. "I'm ready."

I barely heard what he'd just said. I was staring at his right leg. It lay at a horrible angle to the other one, with dry leaves sticking to the hip of his blood-soaked pants.

"Your leg!" I cried out. "Something's wrong with your leg!"

"Get out of here, kid," he snarled. "Get out of here quick!"

I looked up at his face, startled at the harshness of his voice. And again I was gripped by that para-lyzing fear that had stopped me when I first entered the grove.

I can see him yet, as he lay there, facing the Knob, with the six-shooter clutched in his hand. I remem-ber how his nostrils were flared wide and quivering, how his eyes flamed with hate. He wasn't a man any more then; he was a wild animal, trapped and deadly.

"Get, kid!" he snarled again, and I got.

I ran straight through the grove and out on the far side. That's where I saw the saddled horse lying on the ground with a bullet hole through his middle.

Behind me, I heard the chopped-off bark of a six-shooter. Once . . . twice . . . Then from up the slant of Bald Knob, came a strangled shout and the whiplashing report of a rifle. A bullet struck the boulder behind me and went wailing off through the timber.

I hit the cow trail that led toward home, running the fastest I ever ran in my life. I crossed the old laid-out field without ever breaking my stride. If I picked up a single grass bur in my bare feet, I never felt it.

Mama cried that evening when she learned how the law had trailed the wounded Brady Coleman into that china-ball grove and riddled him with bullets.

"What a way for a man to die!" she wept.

"He had it coming to him," Papa said. "He was a bank robber and a killer. There wasn't no good in him."

Maybe Papa was right; I didn't know. But, some-

167

how, the knowledge that Brady Coleman had one time used my china-ball grove for a hide-out made me resent Papa's words.

"What about the treasure?" I asked. "Did they find it?"

"Treasure?" Papa asked. "What treasure?"

I wished then that I hadn't mentioned the treasure. I hadn't told about being in the grove just before the shooting started. It might have reminded Mama of her dominecker rooster.

"If you mean the bank loot," Papa said, "they found it, all right."

My heart sank, then rose again as Papa added: "They found it in his saddle pockets on his dead horse."

So they hadn't found it, after all. Not the *real* treasure. It was still there, and nobody knew where it was buried except me.

It was nearly a week, however, before I could rake up the courage to go back to the grove. It might be haunted now. I knew that lots of places were haunted where a man had been killed. Especially when there was a buried treasure around.

But I found no sign of a ghost when at last I went. All I found was the black stain of the outlaw's blood on top of the rock slab covering his cache.

I lifted the slab and pulled at the lid of the metal box. It came up with a rusty squeak, and I sat staring at Brady Coleman's treasure—a few chipped marbles, a rusty old spur, a Robin Hood book, a ball of fishing cord, and a little white china horse with a rear foot broken off.

For a long time I didn't understand why the sight of that treasure made me cry. Or why I felt compelled to close the lid on it, replace the rock slab, and cover the place with dead leaves.

And even today, I couldn't explain just why I never told another soul about it.

It would have been a thing to brag about, to impress others with—that I was the last to talk to a notorious outlaw before he died. But, for some reason, I never could do it.

I couldn't even tell Jay.

FIFTEEN

That little fast-running possum that Restless Solomon's hounds treed in the big elm that night—we never one time thought he'd cost us half a million dollars and ruin forever Restless's dream of "settling down."

When I brought the possum home in my pocket, he wasn't any bigger than a corncrib rat. But he tamed easy, was a hearty eater, and it wasn't long till he'd filled out and got as big and slick and sassy as a fattening shoat.

I fed him from an old discarded cast-iron skillet and bedded him in a box under the front doorsteps.

I got a lot of pleasure out of watching him gather dry leaves and grass with which to build himself a soft bed inside the box. But once the bed was made, he didn't sleep in it much. Most of the time, he'd come and crawl in bed with me. I'd have to get up extra early on those mornings to keep Mama from catching on that I was sleeping with a possum. She never did, but she did fuss a lot about the amount of possum fur that she thought I brought to bed with me on my clothes.

I called him Scott Cooley, after a famous outlaw that Grandpa Vesper had known back in the Texas Hoodoo War days. This was on account of he was such a scrapper.

I know that possums aren't supposed to fight. At the first hint of danger, they're supposed to fall over and play dead. But Scott Cooley wasn't that kind of a possum. Maybe he'd been pampered too much; I don't know. But any time another animal got to messing around Scott Cooley's feeding pan, trouble started in a hurry.

We learned that one day when Restless came to the house to borrow a hoe. Jay and I were feeding Scott Cooley at the time. One of Restless's hounds was following him. The hound scented the table scraps in Scott Cooley's pan, so he rushed the possum with a growl, aiming to rob him. But it didn't work. Scott Cooley let out a growl just as big and tore into that hound like he meant to eat him alive.

You never saw a worse surprised dog. He'd caught hundreds of possums in his time and had never yet had one to fight back. When he finally fought loose from Scott Cooley, he left out for home in a high run, with his ears laid back and his tail tucked between his hind legs.

I thought Restless would die laughing at that scared dog.

After that, we got to noticing how Scott Cooley would fight anything that bothered him. Restless and Jay were both there the day that one of Papa's work mules got to nosing over the yard fence and overturned Scott Cooley's feed pan. There wasn't any feed in the pan, but it made Scott Cooley mad anyhow. So he set his teeth in the mule's nose and hung with his grip. And the mule was so startled that he reared straight up and fell over backward. You never heard such braying and bawling as that mule put out before he got to his feet again and slung Scott Cooley loose.

"Goshamighty, dang!" Restless said in surprise. "Why, that rascal'll fight you till the cows come home, won't he? Never seen his beat!"

We were all mighty proud of Scott Cooley after

172

that and did considerable bragging about what a scrapper he was.

And that's what finally led us into the big fight.

We were all over at Uncle Adam's mill at Squaw Springs, getting some bread corn ground. Jay was telling the Ishum twins what a fighter Scott Cooley was. They didn't want to believe him.

Cutter Ishum said: "We've got an old brindle housecat I betcha he won't jump on."

I never had liked the Ishum twins. They were too much like their grandpa, old man Tate. On top of that, if you ever got into an argument with one, you had them both to whip. And before Jay came to help me out, I generally wasn't big enough to do it.

Jay said: "You just think he won't. That Scott Cooley possum ain't a-skeered to jump on nothing!"

Cutter's brother Pud said: "If he was to jump on old Brindle, he'd get his plows cleaned. In a hurry, too."

Restless Solomon was standing close by. He heard us arguing and put in. "If that's how you feel about it," he said, "why don't you bring your old cat over for a try?"

And before I quite realized what was happening, Restless had matched a fight for Scott Cooley against the Ishum twins' brindle tomcat, to be held at Restless's house that very night. It happened so fast that it made me sort of uneasy, and after the Ishum twins had left, I turned to Restless.

"You reckon," I said, "that Scott Cooley can handle a big tomcat? Tomcats are sure bad fighters."

"You wait," Restless said. "Scott Cooley can make scrap meat out of any housecat that ever drawed a breath."

I sure did hope so. It would give me a mighty big lift to take those Ishum twins down a notch or two.

Jay and I carried Scott Cooley down to Restless's house that night after supper, taking along the skillet he ate out of and some table scraps to put in it. But when we got there, we found Restless and his woman fixing to drive off in Restless's old rattle-trap of a wagon.

"Boys," Restless apologized, "I'm sure put out with myself. I clean forgot when I matched that fight that I'd promised to play the mouth harp at my woman's brother's wedding tonight. Sure disappoints me, but looks like I'll have to miss out on that cat-and-possum fight."

"You mean we'll have to call it off?" Jay demanded.

"Oh, no," Restless said, climbing into the wagon. "You boys can go right ahead. I've cleaned out that

175

shed room in the back. Put our quail and the mother hen in a box under the kitchen table, where they'll be out of the way. Left you a lamp burning on a table. Be an ideal place to hold that fight, there in that old shed room. . . . Lordy, I sure hate to miss seeing old Scott Cooley tie into that housecat. But you know how a woman is. Thinks her kid brother couldn't get married without I'm there to blow on my mouth harp."

Restless clucked to the horses. "Now, you boys just make yourselves to home," he said, and drove off down the sandy lane.

We went into the shed room where a coal oil lamp sat on a rickety table. We put Scott Cooley on the floor and sat down on a steel-framed cot covered with ragged quilts, and waited till the Ishum twins came.

They brought their brindle housecat tied up in a tow sack. They came in and dumped the sack down in the middle of the floor, and I heard the cat let out a savage growl. We told them where Restless had gone and how he'd let us go on with the fight anyhow.

"All right," Cutter said eagerly. "If y'all are ready, start feeding your possum. We're ready to turn out old Brindle."

Jay put the skillet out in the middle of the floor,

and I emptied the table scraps into it. Scott Cooley
went to the skillet, where he started eating.

Pud went and shut the door, latching it tightly.
"That's so your possum can't run off and get away
the first time old Brindle makes a pass at him," he
said.

Cutter grinned and pulled the sack open. The big
brindle housecat tumbled out into the middle of the
room and started growling.

Sight of him scared me a little. I never saw a bigger tomcat in my life or one that looked any more
vicious. I sort of wished now that I hadn't let Restless match this fight. I didn't want to get Scott
Cooley killed.

The tomcat scented the table scraps Scott Cooley
was eating and started toward him. He walked with
his back arched and his tail all fuzzed up.

Scott Cooley kept eating. If he even knew the cat
was in the room, he didn't let on.

In the lamplight, I could see Jay and the Ishum
twins watching the cat, their eyes lit up with eager
expectancy. I felt my heart leap up and start beating too fast.

Suddenly the cat let out a squawl and sprang. He
landed right on Scott Cooley's back, biting and
clawing, knocking him to the floor.

Scott Cooley squawled too; surprised, I guess.

Then he turned on the cat and they mixed it, snarling and clawing and biting, wrapping themselves around each other and rolling over and over across the floor. They sure had the fur flying.

Jay and I hopped up and down, screaming for Scott Cooley to kill the tomcat. The Ishum twins hopped up and down, screaming just as loudly for Brindle to kill Scott Cooley.

The cat could fight faster than Scott Cooley, but I guess the possum could bite harder. Anyhow, it wasn't but just a little bit before the cat tore loose from Scott Cooley and started circling the room like he was hunting a way out. He was fuzzed up all over now and acting crazy wild, squawling at the top of his voice.

Scott Cooley chased after him, but his pacing run wasn't nearly fast enough to catch the cat.

"Yah! Yah! Scott Cooley's whipped him!" I yelled at Cutter.

"You're a liar," Pud yelled back at me, then busted me one in the nose with his fist.

I felt the blood start and busted Pud right back. Then Cutter swung on me, knocking me down, and Jay yelled, "No, you don't!" and piled into Cutter.

I didn't see it happen because I was on the floor when it took place and Pud was on top of me with his knees in my stomach, beating me in the face with his fists. But I heard the crash, and Jay said later it was him, knocking Cutter clear across the room, that upset the table that held the coal oil lamp.

Anyhow, there was this crash and the sound of glass shattering against the floor. Then a great flash of heat and light filled the room, and the reeking, choking scent of burning coal oil nearly stifled me.

Pud rolled off me and sprang to his feet, screaming at the top of his voice: "*Fire! Fire!*"

I don't remember coming to my feet. All I remember is the four of us standing there in the middle of the room, transfixed with fear, too stunned to do a thing, while a little river of flames crawled under the cot and set fire to the ragged quilts. And I remember, too, how the big brindle housecat leaped right through the flames, which scorched his hair till the yellow smoke boiled up, and how he squawled even louder and leaped up the side of the barc walls and clung there a bit before falling back to go racing around and around the room.

Then Jay came alive and made for the door. He flung it open and yelled back at us. "Come on. We've got to get water!"

I grabbed up Scott Cooley by the tail and made a

dash for the door. I got there at the same time Cutter Ishum did, and we bumped into each other. Neither one could get through. Then Pud ran into us, hitting us so hard that we both landed flat on our backs out on the gallery.

"Find a bucket!" Jay yelled, and I heard the well pulley squealing as he started drawing water.

Out there in the dark, we couldn't see a thing. It was by pure accident that I stumbled over a bucket that Restless had left sitting beside the door. I rushed out with it, Jay filled it, and Cutter snatched it from me and went running with it to the shed-room door. Swinging the bucket high, Cutter hurled its contents into the fire. But all that seemed to do was make the smoke boil up and spread the flames wider and make them leap higher.

We didn't know about pouring water on an oil fire. We drew and dashed bucket after bucket of water into the room. The fire spread all over the room and started climbing the walls. When the flames started spurting up through the cracked shingles, making a wild red flare in the night, terror finally overtook us and we tore out through the darkness, headed for home and help.

Seemed like nearly everybody along Recollection

Creek was gathered around the smoking ruins of Restless's cabin when he and his woman finally arrived. The folks stood silent in the fading glow of the embers, watching Restless as he drove up.

At first, Restless didn't say a word. He just sat there on the spring seat beside his woman, with a puzzled look on his face, like maybe what had happened was too shocking a thing for him to understand. He looked all around, searching the eyes of his neighbors. Then I saw his face gradually take on the solemn look you'd expect to see on a man's face at a time like this.

Papa walked toward Restless and his woman. He said in a nervous, troubled voice: "We'll try to make this good, Restless. Me and my brother Ike and Irv Ishum. It was our younguns that done it, and we ain't wanting to dodge the responsibility."

Restless looked at Papa, then around at Uncle Ike and Irv Ishum. He drew in a long shuddering breath. His face fell to pieces. He started shaking his head and said in a woebegone voice, like he was talking to himself: "Burnt out and ruint. Nary a thing left to make a new start with. Forced to pull up stakes and go on the drift again. Even my hatch of baby quail gone!"

That was the first time I'd thought about our million-dollar hatch of baby quail that Restless said he'd left in a box under the kitchen table. I thought I was already as sick as I could get, but when I remembered the quail, I got sicker.

Restless's words seemed to hit Papa mighty hard, too. His face got a sort of dead white.

Irv Ishum said, "Why, Restless, there ain't no call for you and your woman to leave Recollection Creek. I reckon me and the Creech boys could take turns putting you up till your crop is made and gathered."

Restless climbed down from the wagon, then stood and studied on that proposition for a while.

"No," he said morosely, shaking his head. "We'll hit the road again and try to make out somehow. Ain't no use in hanging on when you know you're done beat. Don't reckon it was meant for me and mine to have nothing, like other folks."

He sucked in another deep, shuddering breath and let it out. "But it's pure hard," he added in a pitiful voice, "having to drive off and leave my crop. Prettiest prospects in the country!"

He lifted sad eyes to look at Papa. Papa looked over at Irv Ishum and then at Uncle Ike. Uncle Ike stared down at the ground.

"Well, all right, Restless," Uncle Ike said, "what do you figure your prospects are worth?"

Restless leaned back against a wagon wheel and stared off up at the stars while he calculated. "Why," he said, "you can't hardly set a fair price on a thing like that, Ike. Something a man's put his soul into and staked his whole future on. Ain't hardly no amount of money can pay for it."

By daylight, Papa and Uncle Ike and Irv Ishum had bought out Restless's crop prospects. They paid him four hundred dollars cash for it. Two hundred more than it was worth, according to Irv Ishum who argued a good long while before he agreed to it. And Irv was nearly right. After he and Papa and Uncle Ike worked the crop out and gathered it, they only got back around three hundred dollars.

As was the custom in those days when somebody had a burn-out, the neighbors all pitched in and loaded Restless's wagon with sacks of corn, bed quilts, bacon, furniture, and clothes till, according to Papa, Restless left Recollection Creek with a wagon piled twice as high as it had been when he came.

Restless accepted the gifts with dignity and solemn thanks.

Just before he started to drive away, he came to where Jay and I stood leaning against a tree, trying to keep as far away from our papas as we could get. I was holding Scott Cooley in my arms. Restless reached out and stroked the possum's singed hair.

"How'd the fight come out?" he whispered.

"All right, I guess," I said nervously.

After setting fire to Restless's house and burning him out, I felt so guilty that I couldn't meet his eyes.

"Knowed it would," he whispered. "Knowed it all the time old Scotty Cooley would eat that tomcat alive."

I looked up, surprised. Restless's voice didn't sound at all like that of a man who'd just suffered a burn-out. It was just as eager and excited as ever.

"Man, oh man! I wish I could have been there to have seen that scrap!" he said.

For a second there, I could have sworn Restless was ready to break out with a big laugh.

But just then Papa walked up and I saw that I'd been wrong. Because, as quick as Restless noticed Papa, his face got sad sober again. And it stayed that way as he turned and walked back toward the loaded wagon. And he walked slow and tired-like, with his shoulders slumped and his feet dragging the ground. Just the way you'd expect a man to walk when hard luck's robbed him of everything he owns and he's forced to go on the drift again.

Even yet, I get an uncomfortable feeling when I think of how Jay and I brought ruin to our friend Restless Solomon.

SIXTEEN

We had it in for old man Tate Ishum, Jay and I did. We resented pretty bitterly all the things he'd done to us—trying to get Grandpa Vesper to whip us, telling on us for swiping that fruit, robbing us of half a million dollars. We figured there ought to be some way we could get back at him and we did considerable thinking on how was the best way to do it. But it seemed like we couldn't come up with a thing that would give us the complete satisfaction we felt we deserved. Not without having to run too big a risk of its backfiring.

As it turned out, I doubt that we could have worked at the problem for the next four or five years and come up with an idea equal to the one that Aaron Blood hatched off for us. That one fixed old man Tate so that we had the ax on him for the rest of his life.

Papa had sold a load of hogs to a man who lived on the other side of Gritville. The day he delivered them Jay and I talked our folks into letting us go along and stay all night with our cousin Lode.

And that happened to be the same day that old man Tate brought to town a whole hackload of ripe watermelons.

We first learned about it when old man Tate came strutting into the newspaper office to get Uncle Gabriel to run a piece in the paper about what early melons he'd raised.

"Earliest in the history of the county," he bragged.

Jay and Lode and I were dumbfounded at the news. In the first place, this was only the middle of June, and nobody ever had ripe melons before the Fourth of July. In the second place, old man Tate had failed to give his usual warning.

We followed him back out to where he'd tied up his mules under the live oak near the town well.

Sure enough, the whole bottom of the hack bed was filled with melons, bedded down in hay to keep them from bruising. They were big melons, too, with rattlesnake stripes down their backs.

A crowd was already gathered; early melons always sold fast, while late ones hardly sold at all.

Old man Tate's gray chin whiskers bristled with fierce importance as folks came up to dicker with him on the price of melons. The look in his little suspicious eyes told you that it would take a smooth customer to slicker him out of anything.

Old man Tate knew all about the selfishness of mankind—he was full of it.

We three boys stood around watching those big melons being carried off. We felt cheated. Always before, when old man Tate had melons about ready to bring in, he'd show up in town a day or so ahead of time, packing a long double-barreled shotgun in the crook of his arm. He'd walk the streets, letting it be known that he was out to get the sneaking underhanded thieves he'd had to run out of his melon patch the night before.

"I'll blow a hole in them a man could pitch a dog through!" he'd threaten.

That was always the tip-off. Lode knew then that old man Tate's patch was ready for raiding, so he'd get word to me. Then Lode and Crawfish Turner and I would get together and make our plans.

Of course, we could have waited a week or so, and there would have been neighbors all over the country with ripe melons we were welcome to. But even after other folks' melons were ripe, we'd lots of times wade right through two or three patches getting to old man Tate's. This was because it seemed like nobody else ever grew melons quite so big and sweet as he did.

But the important raid every year was the first one, which gave us the chance to brag about eating the first melons of the season. So you can see how we felt that day, standing around and watching grown folks get ahead of us.

Some of the men squatted right there in the shade of the big live oak. They wiped the blades of their pocketknives on their pants' legs, cut their melons, and went to eating. They could have offered us some, but they didn't.

After a little while, Crawfish Turner showed up. He came and stood beside me, with his shirttail hanging out, watering at the mouth like the rest of us. Finally, when he could stand it no longer, he eased up closer to the hack.

"Look, Mr. Ishum," he suggested desperately.

"If you was to just happen to drop a little one and bust it or something, could we eat it?"

Jay and I would have known better. We weren't a bit surprised when old man Tate whirled on Crawfish, as vicious as a fighting hog.

"Git!" he shouted. "All of you. Been stealing my melons for years. Seen you in my patch last night. Let me catch you in there agin and I'll blow a hole in you a man could pitch a dog through!"

We left. Not because we thought old man Tate would shoot us, but because we didn't like to be accused of stealing right there in front of all those laughing, melon-eating men.

Sure, we'd swiped watermelons out of the old skinflint's patch. Plenty of times. But that wasn't stealing. Back in those days, nobody along Recollection Creek would have called it *stealing*. Folks just sort of lumped watermelons in the same category with water and air—gifts of God that were free to all. Neighbor ate melons out of neighbor's patch, without bothering to ask. Even a stranger was welcome to a melon. Why, there was no such thing as a watermelon thief.

Not to anybody, that is, except old man Tate Ishum.

But the rankest injustice of all was being accused

190

of raiding old man Tate's patch the night before. That was a flat-out lie. We hadn't even known that he had a melon big enough yet to get pink around the seeds.

We were hidden out under a shed in the wagon yard, suffering the misery of wronged innocence, when Aaron Blood showed up. He came, looking uncomfortable and somehow shy around us, as if he had something to say but wasn't right sure he'd be welcome.

We all stopped talking and stared at him as he came toward us across the wagon yard. That seemed to make him even more nervous. He pulled off the big black hat that he wore. He took out his handkerchief and wiped the inside of it, then wiped his forehead. He took the usual amount of pains to set the hat squarely back on his head. He'd come up and was leaning his heavy shoulders against a cedar post that supported the shed, before he ever got around to looking straight at any of us. Then it was just a short glance, before he stared back down at the broad toes of his shoes. A sheepish sort of grin tugged at the corner of his mouth.

"Look," he said finally. "If y'all boys wouldn't mind having a growed man along, I figure I can help you break that Tate Ishum from sucking eggs!"

Jay didn't have much use for Aaron Blood. He couldn't forget how it was his idea that had won Blood all that horse-race money and that Blood hadn't offered to split with him. Now he stared at Blood in a way to make the big clumsy farmer turn beet red in the face and start fumbling around with his hands, like he couldn't find any place to put them.

Jay said dubiously, "Let's hear what you got in mind."

Jay's stare and the tone of his voice already had Aaron Blood confused. And when the big man started to explain his plan, he stumbled over his words and got worse mixed up than I ever did trying to lie my way out of a whipping. But good as his idea was, it didn't need a lot of explaining.

Even Jay was impressed. He leaped to his feet, with his eyes shining, and started beating a fist into his hand. "That'll do it!" he exclaimed. "That'll itch that old buzzard worse than a bedful of lice!"

Lode ran to the house and swiped some of Uncle Gabriel's clothes—a shirt, a pair of pants, and an old hat. We took them around to the wagon-yard hay shed. Without having to tell too much, we talked old man Jante out of all the hay we needed to stuff the clothes. Then we hid the dummy behind some bales of hay and headed for Uncle Gabriel's house, impatient to get supper over with and be free for the night.

Aaron Blood tagged along after us for a little way, like he wasn't right sure where to go; then he questioned us uneasily. "It'll be all right, won't it? I mean, having a growed man like me along tonight?"

"Sure, if you want to come," Jay said indifferently. "It won't matter none."

I don't think the others noticed that a curious expression came into Aaron Blood's face when he learned that he could go with us. Curious for a man, I mean. It reminded me somehow of the look on a kid's face when somebody's just given him a prize toy that he never hoped to own.

Or it could have been that, like me, the others were so excited over our prospects for adventure that night that they didn't take time to wonder why such an expression would ever show in a man's face.

Old man Tate's sandy-land farm was about a mile from town, and it was a job packing our straw man all the way out there that night. The dummy wasn't heavy, and Aaron Blood carried it; but the straw kept slipping out of the shirt sleeves and the pants' legs, and we'd have to stop and shove it back.

And we needed to hurry, because the moon was fixing to rise and we needed to get our dummy set up before it did.

We made it just barely in time. We climbed up on the slab-rock fence at the far corner of old man Tate's melon patch and looked toward the house. Yellow lamplight glowed through one window.

"He's there, all right!" whispered Crawfish. "We got to be quiet now, or we'll stir up his old hound-dog!"

We hopped down and waded through the lush melon vines. They were dew-damp already and cool to the bare feet of us boys. We stepped mighty careful. We didn't want to maybe trip over a melon and make a lot of racket.

Crawfish whispered to Lode, "You locate us a ripe one to eat while we're waiting."

Anybody can tell a ripe melon in the daytime when he can look for dead curls on the vine or roll a melon over to see if its belly is turning yellow. But it takes a good ear to locate one at night when you've got to depend on thumping. Lode had the best melon-thumping ear in the country.

We set up the dummy on a slight knoll in the middle of the patch. Aaron Blood had brought along a crooked stick that we could run through it and stick into the soft ground. It made the dummy stand in a bent-over position. We made sure that it would stand out well against the moonrise, then went and climbed back over the rock fence.

Lode called softly from a bee-myrtle thicket: "I wasn't sure about the first one, so I brung two."

That suited us. We squatted down in the thicket. Aaron Blood lifted the biggest melon and hammered its bloom-end against the ground. The melon split up the sides, almost as evenly as if he'd cut it with a knife. We'd never seen that done before and commented in surprise, which seemed to please Aaron Blood.

"A busted melon," he explained, "seem like it always tastes better than a knife-cut one."

We crushed the luscious heart of the melon into our mouths and let the juice run off our chins and elbows onto our bare feet. That's the only way to get all the good out of a watermelon; try to be careful with one so that you don't get any juice on you, and something happens to the flavor.

We ate nearly all of the first melon, but didn't try the second. We'd all seen the time when any one of us could have eaten a melon that size. But that was after we'd been eating melons for a week or so. You've got to practice for a couple of weeks, getting your stomach stretched, before you can ever eat enough to amount to much.

The top edge of a big moon sneaked up over the mesquite ridge behind us. When we decided that the moon had risen high enough, we crawled out of the thicket and looked over the rock fence. We'd sure done a good job on the dummy. If we hadn't known better, we'd have been ready to swear there was a man out in that melon patch, stooping to pull a melon.

The light still glowed in old man Tate's window.

Aaron Blood said: "I figure the light's about right now. I'll get him out."

Then he put his hands over his mouth and started squawling and snarling and growling, like a couple of coons fighting over fish heads.

Before he'd finished, old man Tate's hound came alive. He set up a loud baying and headed for the melon patch. A moment later, old man Tate came out into the moonlight. He was running behind the dog.

We moved to where our heads would be hidden in the shadow of a hackberry bush and waited for the fun to start.

Old man Tate came running down to the gate that led into the field. The minute he came through it, he started shouting.

"Git out of them melons, you thieving scum!" he hollered. "Git out of there before I blow a hole in you a man could pitch a dog through."

He came leaping over the melons that we could see shining in the moonlight. He headed straight for the dummy.

"I'm telling you, you better git!" he shouted, waving his long-barreled shotgun. "I said I'd shoot, and I aim to do it!"

Beside me, I could hear Aaron Blood chuckling.

When threats didn't move the melon thief, old man Tate ran up closer, then suddenly stopped and brought up his gun.

"Done give my last warning!" he shouted and cut loose with both barrels.

Two long streams of fire reached out toward the dummy. The blast stirred up echoes a mile away.

The twin loads of shot must have caught the dummy dead center. We saw it jerk and sort of fling up its arms like a falling man would, then pitch sideways to the ground.

The sight made a little cold chill run up my spine. What if that had been one of us?

I guess something like the same thought must have struck old man Tate. He stood in his tracks, staring at his kill, then suddenly exclaimed in an awed voice: "Dangamighty! Gosh, dangamighty!"

He wheeled then and headed for the house, running as hard as he could go. He tripped over a melon, fell down, got up, then seemed to run faster than ever.

We laughed till we were sick. We kept it quiet because we didn't want old man Tate to catch on; but, inside, we were shouting and laughing at the tops of our voices.

Finally Lode said, "Well, I guess we can go now."

"No, wait," Aaron Blood said. "We got the britches scared off that old fool. He thinks he's done a killing."

Almost before he'd finished talking, we heard the clatter of hoofs coming down the lane from the house. It was old man Tate. He'd saddled a horse and was headed for town.

He raced past our hiding place, whipping over and under, riding the wildest you ever saw.

"It's getting better all the time," Aaron Blood said. "He's a-going after somebody. Let's wait and see who he brings back."

In less than an hour, old man Tate was back, bringing Sheriff Dave Hawkins and old Doc Grandberry with him. The sheriff and Doc came in a buggy. They left the buggy at the fence and came hurrying through the melons. Old man Tate was trotting at their heels like a nervous fice dog.

"He's laying right up yonder on that little rise," he was chattering. "I didn't aim to do it, Sheriff. I just lost my temper and cut down on him before I thought."

Doc grunted. The sheriff didn't say anything.

"What'll they do, Sheriff?" old man Tate demanded. "What stand will the law take on this? I tell you it was just sort of an accident! I never really meant it a'tall!"

The sheriff said: "Well, if you've kilt him, Tate, it's liable to go hard with you. Folks in this country don't look on a stole melon as a killing matter."

"But dang it!" the old man shrilled resentfully. "Ain't a man got no rights? Can't he pertect his lawful-owned property?"

They were right at the fallen dummy now, and old man Tate stopped, hanging back. He kept looking everywhere, except at the body. I guess he didn't want to see it.

The sheriff and Doc reached down to turn the corpse over. Then both straightened and stared at each other. A second later, Doc threw back his head, and you could have heard his bawling laugh a mile off.

That startled old man Tate. He backed off a couple of steps. "What is it?" he demanded. "Ain't he dead yet?"

Doc Grandberry bawled louder. Sheriff Hawkins sank down to squat on his boot heels, where he rocked and roared.

Old man Tate kept staring at them. "Dang it!" he complained. "What is it? What've y'all found?"

He moved cautiously forward and finally raked up enough nerve to bend down and peer at the corpse.

"Dangamighty!" he yelped suddenly. He snatched up the dummy and let it fall. "I've been tricked. Somebody's made a fool out of me!" He fought the night air with his fists. "Why, dangamighty. If I knowed who the scoun'ls was, I'd blow a hole in 'em that a man could pitch a dog through!"

"Wait till Gabriel Creech gets hold of this," bawled Doc Grandberry. "Won't he make his *Horn* blare with it? He'll spread it all over the front page."

That stopped old man Tate so quick that he still held one fist in the air. He let it fall.

"Doc," he pleaded. "Doc, you can't do that to me. If you let this get into *Gabriel's Horn,* it'll ruin me. I'll get laughed clean out of the country."

He waited for Doc's laughter to run out, then started begging in earnest.

"Look," he whined. "I'm an old man. Too old to stand being laughed at for the rest of my life. We could keep this quiet, if you would. Just between the three of us. I'll pay you for your trip out, Doc. I'll make it right with you, Sheriff. But, for gosh sake, don't let that fool Gabriel Creech put this in his paper and ruin me. Not an old man like me."

Old man Tate was sure telling it sad. He was even crying a little bit when he finally talked Doc and the sheriff into a promise.

We waited till they were gone. Then Jay caught me around the neck. I hugged Lode, and he hugged Crawfish. Finally, we all rolled on the ground and laughed till the tears came.

All except Aaron Blood. He just sat there, with his broad back braced against the rock fence, chuckling a little. Then, after a while, he reached for the second melon and broke it against the ground, splitting it up the sides as evenly as he had the first one.

A story like we had was the kind Uncle Gabriel liked best. And if we'd given it to him, he really would have browned old man Tate's goose to a turn. But we held out on him. This was on account of an idea Jay had.

We managed to all make it into town the next Saturday when old man Tate brought in another load of melons and we all went over and offered to buy one.

"Let's see your money first," old man Tate snapped. He sure did look raw-edged and jumpy about something or other.

"Let's see the melon first," Jay countered. "We don't want to eat no melon with blood on it."

Old man Tate jerked like he'd been stabbed with a knife. "Blood!" he yelped. "What about blood?"

"I mean," Jay said, "that when you take to shooting down people all over a melon patch, you're bound to spatter blood on some of the melons."

The old man's face turned purple. I never saw such a wild, crazy look come into a man's eyes.

"That confounded Doc Grandberry!" he burst out. "I knowed he was lying when he said he wouldn't tell it around."

"It ain't been told around," Jay said. "Not yet. Uncle Gabriel hasn't even got it for his paper—yet."

Old man Tate's mouth fell open. He stared at Jay. He turned and stared at me and Lode and Crawfish. Suddenly, his bristling chin whiskers wilted.

"All right," he muttered. "You've got me over the big barrel. Take your melon. Keep your money. Go visit my patch when you get ready. But don't let that story get into *Gabriel's Horn*."

He was trembling all over when he lifted out a melon for us.

202

We felt mighty smug while we ate it.

But the next time we raided old man Tate's patch, something was wrong. Nobody knew what it was. Nobody even mentioned it. But I think every one of us realized even then that we'd never go back. For some curious reason, old man Tate's melons seemed to have lost their extra-special flavor.

We were all grown men, I guess, before we ever realized what went with it.

SEVENTEEN

I don't recollect just how long Grandpa was laid up from taking that load of turkey shot in his backside, but I know it was a long long time. And even after he was able to leave his bed, he still wasn't able to do anything much except stomp around the house and fret and complain about everything from Grandma's cooking to the state of the weather.

Grandma understood how frustrated and helpless an active man can feel when he's tied to the house. She did everything she could to pacify Grandpa. While firmly convinced that the old man suffered in payment for the sin of turkey shooting over the graves of her dead people, Grandma was careful never to say so and did her best to talk Grandpa into a more reasonable frame of mind.

"Now, Vesper, don't fret so," she'd say. "You can't expect a tail end that's as old and thin and bony as yourn to heal overnight, like it was young and fat. You'll be back in the saddle soon enough."

But it wasn't soon enough for Grandpa. And I guess it was just barely soon enough for Grandma. Because I remember that she didn't complain any the morning that Grandpa had me and Jay corral that *grulla* dun horse he'd had to put off breaking to the saddle on account of his wounds.

The dun was a three-year-old with a lot of fire in his eye. He showed fight the instant that Grandpa roped him.

Generally, Grandma put up a big fuss any time Grandpa got to fooling with a young horse, claiming he was too old and beat up now to mess with the bad ones. But this morning she kept quiet. She stood outside the pole corral, twisting her bonnet strings around her hands while Grandpa threw the dun. She watched him roll the animal into the saddle and tighten the cinch. She got a little white in the face when he released the ropes from the dun's feet and stepped across the saddle as the horse came lunging up, bawling and pitching. And when the outraged dun finally reared up on his hind legs, and Grandpa had to hand him one between the ears with the butt end of his quirt to keep the dun from coming back over on him, I heard Grandma gasp and saw her whirl and run for the house.

But as frightened for Grandpa as she must have been, she still didn't argue one bit against his going ahead and finishing the breaking job.

"I don't like it," I heard her telling Aunt Severance a couple of days later. "But I tell you there's nothing as nerve-frazzling to a woman as having to put up with a sickly man around the house."

I always suspected, too, that Grandma harbored a secret hope that Grandpa would take enough interest in his horsebreaking to forget his turkey hunting. But if she did, it was wasted hope.

As soon as Grandpa got the dun gentled down enough that he wouldn't fall to pieces every time a stick popped under his feet, the old man began taking long rides in the pasture. And on every trip, he packed his Winchester in his saddle scabbard. He didn't say so, but anybody who knew him knew that he was hunting that big gobbler again.

Grandma knew it and cried about it, seeming, in some mystic way, to have foreknowledge of the tragic end that lay in wait for Grandpa. But, by the same sense, she apparently realized the futility of pleading with him to let that gobbler alone. So she cried in secret, mourning his loss even before she lost him.

When Grandpa finally caught sight of the big gobbler again, it was just as he and the dun topped out a high ridge north of the Scallon burial lot. Before him, beyond a brushy dry wash, a long gentle slant of ground led up to a cedar-combed ridge. The slope was all open except for a scattering of catclaw.

And about halfway up the slope was the gobbler.

The big bird hadn't seen or heard Grandpa, so he wasn't spooked yet. He was just walking casually along, his blue head bobbing backward and forward on his long neck in slow rhythm to the steps he took.

It was a perfect setup. The sun was at Grandpa's back, its rays striking fire from the bird's burnished bronze back. The gobbler was less than a hundred yards away and had more than another hundred yards of open ground to traverse before he could reach cover.

Let the rascal see Grandpa now; it didn't matter. Let him run or fly; it was all the same. At last, Grandpa had that tricky old bird out in the open where he could get a fair chance at him.

Grandpa piled down out of the saddle, dragging his Winchester from the scabbard. He jacked a cartridge into the firing chamber. It was in his mind to stick a bullet right where that gobbler's wings were hinged to his back.

But the dun couldn't see it that way. The rattle of the gun as Grandpa loaded it was too much for the spook-hunting bronc. He snorted and fell against the reins, dragging Grandpa back down the slant.

Grandpa yelled at him, finally wheeled to run and plant a couple of solid kicks in the dun's ribs. But of course, by that time, it was too late. The gobbler had heard or sighted them and instantly streaked for cover.

When Grandpa finally dragged the protesting dun to the top of the ridge again where he could see over, his gobbler was just a flash of brown disappearing into the cedars.

Grandpa was pretty riled about losing that shot. He stepped back across the saddle and bogged his spurs deep into the dun's ribs. He all but lifted that snorting bronc down the slant and up the next without giving the animal's hoofs a chance to touch the ground.

The gobbler was frightened and running now, but if Grandpa could get to the top of that cedar ridge in time, he still had a good enough chance to get a shot.

Sure enough, when they crashed through the cedars on the far side of the second ridge, yonder went the gobbler. He was toeing it off at a fast clip across a wide prickly-pear flat.

Grandpa reached for his gun a second time. But now there was no stopping the dun. He'd been spurred into a panic and had gone wild. This happened to be the first time that Grandpa had ever ridden him without a hackamore, and there was no holding him with the bridle. He'd clamped the bits between his teeth and was running cold-jawed and blind.

The gobbler flew at the sight of them. He whipped himself heavily into the air and sailed off across the flat, gliding on wide-spread wings barely above the prickly pear.

Finding that he couldn't hold the dun, Grandpa decided that the next best thing was to let the fool horse run. Which he did. He slacked off on the reins and reached for his hat. Leaning forward in the saddle, he yelled in the dun's ear and started whipping him over the head with his Stetson. By changing sides of the dun's head, Grandpa managed to keep the runaway fought out of the worst brush thickets and headed in the same general direction as the gobbler.

Grandpa was stirred up now bound and determined to get his turkey.

Running as fast as he was, the dun wasn't too far behind when the bird hit the ground. And by spurring harder and yelling louder, Grandpa forced his wildly running mount into an extra burst of speed that crowded the gobbler back into the air again before they were out of the prickly pear.

The second flight wasn't so far. The gobbler was a heavy bird and tired fast on the wing. The third flight, which carried him to the crest of a low brushy ridge, was less than a hundred yards.

After that, the gobbler didn't fly any more. But there was still plenty of run left in his long legs. He tore out down the bed of a dry-water course, traveling like a bronze streak.

Behind him, Grandpa's dun had run far enough to be done with his scare. He was ready to stop any time now.

But Grandpa wouldn't have it. He shoved his Winchester back into its scabbard and reached for his catch rope.

"You was aching to run, dang you," he growled at the dun, "so bow your neck and have at it."

He started reefing the runaway down one hind leg and then the other with his rope to encourage him.

The sting of that rope flattened the dun under the saddle and started him to stretching out for all he could reach. The gap between him and the running gobbler began to close.

There was a strip of blackjack timber just ahead, but Grandpa rode onto the gobbler before they reached it. He leaned out of his saddle. He whirled the loop of his hard-twist rope over his head one time. Then he whipped it against the gobbler's outstretched neck, aiming to break it.

The gobbler rolled in the grass, loose wings pinwheeling, then flopped over on his breast, to lie there quivering.

"By gum, I guess I got him that time!" Grandpa shouted jubilantly and hauled back on the reins.

The dun squatted and slid to a halt, happy for the chance to stop running now. He stood spraddle-legged and blowing, all the scare run out of him, while Grandpa swung down to get his turkey. The bronc was so winded that he didn't even flinch when Grandpa flopped the turkey's limber neck across the saddle and looped an offside saddle string below the gobbler's head.

Grandpa felt mighty satisfied with himself when he mounted again. Here he'd finally managed to get his gobbler, and at the same time, run a lot of fret and foolishness out of the dun. He swung the bronc toward home, willing to bet the animal wouldn't be hunting any more spooks to scare at that day.

And that's when the stunned gobbler came to life.

One moment Grandpa was riding along, thinking turkey-and-dressing; the next, the turkey was climbing up into his face and whipping him blind with heavy blows of his strong wings.

Grandpa had his bronc figured to be run off his feet, but he was mistaken. At the first move of the gobbler, the dun snorted, swallowed his head, and quit the earth. He bawled like a choking calf. He rolled in the air and sunned the left side of his belly. He came down, one foot at a time, giving Grandpa four separate jolts. He went up a second time, shaking himself like a dog leaving water, and gave the sun a chance at his right side.

Grandpa had never been a man to brag on his riding, but the rest of us Creeches would. It wasn't in any of us to try to conceal the fact that Grandpa could ride any hair-growing creature he could get a leg across. But of course, he couldn't be expected to do it with a wild turkey gobbler spurring him in the face.

That gobbler flustered Grandpa. He lost one stirrup the second jump. The third jump snapped him clear of the saddle. He sailed out over a wild persimmon bush, clutching a wad of the dun's mane in one fist and a handful of turkey feathers in the other. He landed head-on against the base of a blackjack oak, and that blacked him out.

It was nearly noon when the dun showed up at the corrals with an empty saddle. By the middle of the afternoon, half the men and boys along Recollection Creek were out hunting Grandpa. The womenfolks stayed at the house, gathering around Grandma Elfie and comforting her with recollections of all the broken and mangled bodies of riders that bad horses had thrown and dragged to death.

Nobody found Grandpa. He made it in to the house by himself, just about dark. His hat was gone and his head was bloody, and both glasses had been knocked out of his steel-rimmed spectacles. Otherwise, he seemed all right. He did act mighty worn out, but that was to be expected of a man who was never known to walk a step that a horse could pack him.

He came in and sat down on the front gallery. He complained some of his head aching, and couldn't quite seem to understand why all the folks were gathered and making such a to-do over him. But after Grandma had brought him a tin cup of medicine, he perked up and told what had happened. And after he inquired and learned that the dun had come in all right, he seemed to get as big a laugh as anybody out of the scrape he'd got into.

"Me and that old graveyard gobbler's had our rounds," he said, grinning, "but, by gum, I got him at last. Elfie can have him oven-baked and stuffed with onion dressing by moonrise, if you folks'll all lay over for the feed."

A short silence took hold of everybody when Grandpa said that. Then Uncle Ike broke out with sudden laughter.

"But, Pa," Uncle Ike said, "there wasn't a sign of a turkey on that dun horse when he come in."

Grandpa started. I remember yet how his old head lifted up in the lamplight, turning from side to side on his scrawny neck like a steer that's scented blood.

"No turkey!" he exclaimed. "Why, I had a saddle string hog-knotted around that gobbler's neck. He couldn't have got away!"

Uncle Ike's laughter got louder. "But, Pa, he did. Somehow, that rascal managed to run another whizzer on you!"

Uncle Ike's laughing brought on more, and several of the men slapped their legs and roared.

But Grandpa didn't laugh. And Grandma Elfie didn't, either. Grandma said afterward she didn't guess anybody else saw the look that came into Grandpa's face when he learned that gobbler had given him the slip for the third time. Leastways, they never mentioned it.

But Grandma saw it and said it was the sort of look that made her want to scream. She always declared that one look told her that her man was doomed, that that graveyard gobbler had got him at last.

But a body has to bear up in times like that, Grandma explained. A woman can't afford to break down and carry on in a way to shame her man. So she held her hurt and fear inside her.

Grandpa didn't say anything for a good little while. He just sat silent and seemed to start shrinking away inside. And pretty soon, while folks were still laughing, Grandpa reached up and gripped a gallery post and pulled himself slowly to his feet.

"I'll go rest up a spell," he said a strained voice. "I feel sort of porely."

And those, according to Grandma Elfie, were Grandpa's last mortal words.

I remember listening to the clink and drag of his spur rowels as he walked haltingly into the room where he slept and how loud the bedsprings creaked when he threw himself across the quilts.

Grandma heard the same thing and said later she wanted to follow him right then, but she had her good-bys and thank-yous to make to all the folks. Then when finally the last one of us had left and she hurried to her man, she found the bed empty and Grandpa gone!

Grandma couldn't hold back her screams any longer then. She flung her apron up over her face, and it was a thick heavy one, made out of a salt sack; but even through it, some folks said they heard her screams half a mile away in the dark.

Anyhow, we all went back. And we searched the house and searched the corrals and barn and every other place we could think of that Grandpa might have wandered off to. We even spread out, packing lighted lanterns through the woods, hoping we'd come upon him. But it wasn't till nearly sunup the next morning that Papa and Uncle Wiley finally located him.

He was in the old Scallon burial lot. They found him slumped down behind Great-grandpa Mill-Wheel Scallon's grave. His rifle lay across the tombstone and in his clenched right hand was gripped his hollow-bone turkey caller.

Finding Grandpa dead at a turkey roost was enough to throw us all. But the thing about it that gave us such an odd, creepy feeling was the litter of green leaves that lay all around his body. All had been cut and squared up like Restless Solomon and others trimmed their leaves for calling turkeys.

There was even one in the roof of Grandpa's open mouth, held in place by the tip of his tongue!

In those days, folks didn't go in much for fancy funerals. A man could die and be buried without the bother and expense of a satin-lined casket, big mounds of bought hothouse flowers, and a paid preacher to pray over his remains.

The Savage boys came with their saws and hammers. When they couldn't find any more suitable lumber, they knocked a feed trough apart and built Grandpa a coffin out of the pieces.

Aaron Blood dug the grave, and Ruel MacLaurin came and helped him. And Uncle Ike got pretty bitter about Ruel's doing it. Uncle Ike said that was just a cheap and underhanded way Ruel had of buttering up and taking the advantage. He said that pretty-boy bronc rider was just sly enough to know that you couldn't get away with shooting a man who's helping to dig your father's grave.

They dug the grave under the big old live oak in the corner of the Scallon burial lot. And that's where we all gathered and sang and cried and prayed and finally laid Grandpa Vesper to rest—right beside the bones of Grandma's people that Grandpa had tromped over while he turkey-hunted.

I know now that my Grandpa Vesper must have died from a brain concussion suffered when the *grulla* dun threw him against the base of that black-jack tree. I'm certain that the injury to his brain brought on a temporary mental derangement which caused the old man to go back down to the turkey roost that night and try to call turkeys by the green-leaf method. And of course, there is a perfectly logical explanation of each of Grandpa's previous and unfortunate experiences with that wild gobbler.

Yet, during the funeral, while we were lowering Grandpa's body into the grave and some of the women were trying to sing "The Last Call" in grief-stricken voices, there occurred a thing for which I've never found a logical and satisfactory answer and no longer expect to.

It was Grandpa's graveyard gobbler. I know it

was, because of the monstrous size of the bird and because of the patches of gray feathers at his wing tips. He appeared on top of a high ridge above the graveyard. In the face of all our crying and singing, he showed himself in a bald patch of ground, where he boldly fanned his tail and gobbled and strutted and drummed with his wings till the last clod was piled on Grandpa's grave.

Don't try to tell me that a thing like that was pure coincidence. It was too shocking, too preposterous, too weirdly awesome. I remember yet the sudden hush that fell upon the burial party when that happened, the frightened glances that were exchanged, and how quickly we all hurried away from the grave, glancing nervously back over our shoulders as we went.

Later on, I heard Grandma Elfie's one mention of that happening, spoken in a voice full of heartbreak, yet with a touch of bitterness and resentment. "I tell you," she said, "there's the natural things of this world, and then there's the unnatural. And stomping around over the bodies of dead people, trying to shoot a turkey, is contrary to nature."

Which probably comes about as close to the truth of the matter as anybody will ever get.

EIGHTEEN

Sis's secret romance with Ruel MacLaurin went on so long without anything coming of it that Aunt Minnie got worried. Jay and I heard her complaining to Sis about it a couple of weeks after Grandpa's funeral.

They were inside the kitchen at the time, cooking wild plum jelly. Jay and I were just outside in the yard, squatted in the shade of a china-ball tree. We were whittling some new slingshot stocks out of forked persimmon branches.

The only way Jay could do any good whittling with a pocketknife was to stick his tongue out of one corner of his mouth and chew on it while he worked.

And of course, he couldn't talk while he was chewing on his tongue; and with Jay not talking, I didn't have anything to say, either. We'd been busy like that for a good long while. And that's how come Sis and Aunt Minnie didn't realize anybody was around to hear what they talked about.

Aunt Minnie said, "Honey, I'm getting bothered about you and Ruel. I don't like for you to keep slipping off and meeting him out away from the house like that. It looks bad."

"I know, Mama," Sis agreed. "But I don't know what else to do. You know how Papa is!"

"Nobody knows better," Aunt Minnie said. "I've talked with that man till I'm black in the face. But for all the good I've done, I might just as well have been trying to dip water with a tea strainer. When it comes to cantankerous stubbornness, I'd pick your daddy ahead of a mule any time."

They were silent for a while, then Aunt Minnie went on in an uneasy voice. "Ruel's a fine, handsome young man, and I'd be proud for you to have him. But I'd druther see you give him up than to go on meeting him in secret like this."

"But, Mama!" Sis said, her voice lifted in alarm. "I can't give him up. You know I can't!"

Aunt Minnie said worriedly, "I was afraid maybe you wouldn't. That's what's got me bothered sick."

There's no telling how long Aunt Minnie might have had to go on worrying about Sis and Ruel if Uncle Ike's well hadn't gone dry.

It was curious about that well. Nobody ever could explain what happened to it. One day it was furnishing all the water anybody could ask for; then the next morning when Aunt Minnie went out to draw up some breakfast water, all she got was about half a bucket of ooze and settlings.

Uncle Ike wouldn't believe it. He pointed out that there hadn't been any extra amount of water drawn out of that well in months, that there'd been plenty of rainfall to keep up the water level, and that he hadn't felt any landshifting earthquake that might cut off or dam up the underground streams. Therefore, he said, there still had to be water in that well.

But when he went out to prove it to Aunt Minnie, he came up with the same answer she had—that the well had gone dry.

That made Uncle Ike pretty mad and he stomped around the yard, shouting and taking on nearly as bad as he had the day that Ruel MacLaurin whipped Jay. But after a while, he got so thirsty for a drink that he let Aunt Minnie and Sis talk him into hitching the mules to the wagon and hauling water from the creek.

He hauled the water in a couple of empty vinegar

barrels. He'd been keeping them to store pecans in when he threshed his trees in the fall. He got it out of the spring that fed the old baptizing hole, which was the nearest place for him to get clean drinking water.

I happened to go over to Uncle Ike's right after dinner that day and got there in time to go after the second load. I had my new slingshot with me and Jay had his, and while Uncle Ike was hitching up the mules, Jay and I visited a special place behind the barn where a hill slope was littered with brown sandstone rocks that were nearly round and just the right size for shooting in a slingshot. We filled our pockets with this ammunition because Jay had figured out how nice it would be to shoot game while we rode along in a wagon, instead of having to hunt afoot.

And it worked out pretty good for Jay. Seemed like he could stand in the bed of that jostling wagon and shoot about as straight with his slingshot as he could with his feet on the ground. I remember how, just as we drove away from the barn, I saw a chaparral bird skin out from the feed lots and race toward the brush. The chaparral had just robbed a chicken hen's nest and was still carrying an egg stuck on his long beak.

I said, "Looky yonder!" and cut down on the chaparral with my slingshot and missed. But Jay's shot, which came just a second after mine, was so close that it broke the egg off the bird's beak. You never saw a chaparral do such crazy spinning around and hopping and wing flopping as that one did before he got straightened out and took to cover.

We shot at some cottontails, and Jay cut hair out of the back of one of them. But seemed like I wasn't so steady on my feet as Jay was; I missed every time.

Uncle Ike sat slumped in the spring seat, paying no attention to us. He rode with his head down, sad about Grandpa's dying, I guessed, or maybe worried about his well going dry. Then Jay shot too close to one of the mules. He was trying for a squirrel that was racing through the grass toward a big oak tree. The mule snorted and shied against the other one.

Uncle Ike came alive then and whirled on us.

"If you younguns monkey around and scare these mules into a run, I'll tear your tail ends up worse than a wild sow's bed!"

It scared me, how mad Uncle Ike got so quick. But Jay just said "Yessir," and waited till Uncle Ike had turned back around. Then he winked at me and grinned.

Then before the grin faded, I saw his eyes widen and take on that look of devilment that nearly always got us into trouble.

"Looky yonder!" he breathed in a whisper.

I looked the way he was looking. Up ahead, right beside one of the mules now, was a nest of yellow wasps hanging in a turkey-pear bush. That nest was big as a Mexican's straw hat and must have had a million wasps clinging to it.

"Watch me get it!" he bragged in a whisper.

I don't know yet whether Jay didn't think, or just didn't care what he was doing. I opened my mouth to say "No!" but I was too late. Jay had already let fly.

It was the most perfect shot I ever saw made. It had to have been an accident. Not even Jay was good enough to shoot in two the inch-long stem that held the nest to the bush.

But that's what happened. The nest tumbled to the ground—and up rose a yellow cloud of the angriest wasps you ever saw!

The wasps swarmed over us, stabbing us so fast with red-hot stingers that there wasn't time to think what to do.

Uncle Ike jumped to his feet and hollered "Dang-amighty!" and went to fighting wasps with both hands. Then the mules jumped and snorted and jerked the wagon so hard that I lost my balance and fell down, banging my head against a barrel just as it bounced out over the tail gate.

I came to my feet, hopping and yelling, and up front Uncle Ike was hollering, "Whoa, mules! Whoa, now!"

But the wasps were stinging the mules, too, and they wouldn't listen to Uncle Ike. They were rearing and plunging and wringing their tails, each trying to go off in a different direction.

Then they finally got together on it, the mules did, and quit the road, and here we went yonder.

The wagon bounced and crashed and tore through the brush. It rode down big pole saplings that splintered and cracked and slammed against the underside of the wagon as they sprang back in place. Dead wood popped and sticks and leaves came whizzing through the air.

It was sure a wild ride we took while we howled and fought wasps. One wheel hit a boulder, bouncing the tail end of the wagon so high that I fell down again. And when I finally struggled up on my all fours, so I could look, I saw that Jay and the second barrel were gone.

I thought the runaway would never stop. But it

finally did—when the mules ran right off that high dirt bank and jumped headfirst into the baptizing hole.

They took the wagon with them, of course, and I don't know how to tell what it felt like, riding that plunging wagon through the air.

The mules hit the water first and went under. The wagon crashed down on top of them. Then a big splash of water blinded and swept over me, and I knew that I was drowning.

When the water cleared away, though, I found that it wasn't me who was drowning. It was Uncle Ike. He'd gone overboard into that deep water. He was splashing and hollering and calling for help and grabbing frantically at the side of the wagon bed.

I reached out and put his hand on the sideboard and watched him grunt and strain and cough as he pulled himself to safety. Then I looked up and saw the mules. They were climbing out on the far bank.

But they weren't taking us out with them. All they were hooked to now was the wagon's running gear, which had sunk from under us.

There we were—Uncle Ike and I—floating around in a loose wagon bed, out in the middle of that deep, dangerous baptizing hole. Same as in a boat.

Only it wasn't exactly the same, either; because a boat is supposed to hold the water out, and our wagon bed wasn't. All around its edges and up between the floorboards, the water was coming in. Not fast, but it was coming.

Uncle Ike knelt in the wagon bed and dripped water and stared pop-eyed at the mules that had come to a stop after they'd tried to go around a big mesquite tree, each to a different side. Then suddenly he whirled and was gripping my shoulder so tight that it hurt.

"Jay!" he said in a wild voice. "Where's my baby boy Jay?"

I shook my head; I wasn't up to talking yet.

Uncle Ike got to his feet and ran to the back end of the wagon box, making the front end rise. He bent over and tried to look down into the deep water. He started moaning and crying.

"My pore little baby boy," he wept. "Drowned in a baptizing hole!"

My breath finally came, and I said: "He's not drowned. He's not even in the water. He fell out back yonder somewhere."

Uncle Ike turned and stared at me like he couldn't understand.

"He's back yonder somewhere," I repeated, pointing the way we'd come. "Him and the barrels. They fell out back yonder with the wasps."

That broke Uncle Ike down completely. "Praise the Almighty!" he exclaimed. "My baby boy, he's saved."

He looked down then and saw the water spurting up through the floorboards. He stared at it appalled, then turned to me, white in the face and with his lips trembling.

"Hop," he said in an awed voice, not much louder than a whisper. "We're sinking, Hop. Pray if you can, boy. Thank the good Lord that my baby boy is saved from this watery grave."

I wasn't so strong on praying right then. I was too put out with Jay. I would just as soon that it was him instead of me fixing to drown. After all, he was the one who had shot down the wasp nest.

Suddenly I felt salt tears stinging my eyes and was overcome with a rush of bitter resentment. It didn't seem fair for me to have to drown while Jay got off scot-free!

Then I heard brush snapping and dragging against saddle leather. It was Ruel MacLaurin riding up. He'd come to see Sis, I guess, but had found us instead.

Sight of Ruel set my heart to jumping. I suddenly wanted to laugh. Ruel would save us!

But Ruel didn't go about saving us in much of a hurry. He just rode up to the edge of the water and lifted a leg to crook it around his saddle horn. Then he grinned at us and started rolling a cigarette.

Uncle Ike stared at him for a moment, then went to jumping up and down. "Well, confound it!" he raged at Ruel. "Don't just set there grinning like a briar-biting mule. Get us out of here."

Ruel lit his cigarette and lifted one eyebrow. "I'd druther dicker a little first."

Uncle Ike's mouth fell open. Then his face got black. "Dicker," he roared. "With the lives of a man and boy at stake? Why, if I had my Winchester, I'd—"

"Sure," Ruel put in. "You'd plant a ball right between my eyes. . . . But you ain't got that Winchester this time, little man. And that wagon box is settling fast."

Uncle Ike stood stock still while the water bubbled up around his feet. He couldn't even speak. All he could do was stand there with his mouth open.

Finally his chin started shaking. "All right, con-

found you!" he said. "You win. I'll forget the shooting."

"Well, now, that's fine," Ruel said. "But how about me and Sis? We're sort of bent on getting married."

"Married!" screamed Uncle Ike. "I'll drown first. I'll—"

Then he slumped and looked around at me. "No," he said, brokenly, shaking his head. "That won't do. A man can't let his wants cost the life of his brother's son."

Ruel laughed and winked at me. "Now don't let Hop's safety influence you none. Hop can swim out any time he takes a notion. He and your baby boy, they've been swimming in this hole all spring!"

A grasshopper could have kicked me out of that wagon bed right then. I'd been so scared that I'd completely forgotten that Jay and I both had learned to swim that spring.

Uncle Ike started jumping up and down again, splashing the water in the rapidly sinking wagon bed.

"You mean," he said, "that devilish Jay's been risking his life in this dangerous hole—after I told him not to?"

233

"All spring long," Ruel said. "Could have drowned himself a dozen times."

"Get me out of here," Uncle Ike shouted. "I'll learn that hard-headed scamp to listen to what his papa says. Hurry up and get me out of here."

Ruel said: "What about me and Sis?"

"Well, what about it?" stormed Uncle Ike. "If you want her, take her. But get me out of here. I aim to frazzle that Jay's tail till he'll eat standing up for a solid month!"

Ruel laughed out loud. "I sure want to see that done," he said.

He took down his catch rope and pitched it to us.

We didn't have much trouble in locating Jay. We just followed back along the opening that the runaway had knocked in the brush till we heard his hollering. We found him trapped under an overturned vinegar barrel, with a fallen tree trunk lying across the top, pinning the barrel to the ground. Jay was sure hollering loud. There were some mad wasps trapped in the barrel with him, and he didn't have enough elbow room to fight them.

Ruel shoved the tree trunk off the barrel and tipped it over. Jay leaped out, and Uncle Ike collared him.

"Ruel," Uncle Ike said, "would you give me the loan of that rawhide quirt on your saddle?"

"Why, it'll pleasure me, Mr. Creech," Ruel said. "It sure will."

He got his quirt off his saddle, and Uncle Ike took it and frazzled Jay's tail for him, just like he'd threatened.

Jay pitched and hollered and squawled, but Uncle Ike held to his collar and worked him over till he and Ruel both seemed satisfied. Then he turned Jay loose and watched him take to the brush, still hollering bloody murder.

"Now, Ruel," Uncle Ike said, "that'll give you some idea of how to handle them devilish little scamps you and Sis are bound to raise."

Then Uncle Ike did a thing I never would have believed of a man with his temper. He turned and slapped Ruel MacLaurin on the shoulder like Ruel was his best friend. Then he threw back his head and started laughing at the top of his voice.

Just as if the whole thing had been a big joke.

I took out after Jay. Sometimes it seemed like Uncle Ike was harder to figure out than his baby boy was.

NINETEEN

Sis and Ruel MacLaurin got married at Grandma Elfie's house. This was partly because Grandma had more room, but mostly because Uncle Ike had got word that heavy rains were falling on his Coke County farm again and he was fixing to move back there. And what with trying to get all their belongings packed for the trip, Aunt Minnie had the house too torn up for anybody to get married in.

I remember a number of remarkable things that happened at that wedding.

I remember how Silas Savage set out to kiss the

bride before she was a bride. And when folks kept holding him off, Silas finally got loud and wanted to fight, and his brother Thurman and Uncle Adam Creech caught him and shut him up in the smokehouse and wired the door shut with baling wire. Silas tried to climb out through the little breeze window, high up in the gable end of the house, and got stuck there and kept yelling at the top of his voice. Not yelling to be helped down, but for somebody to please lift the bride up within kissing reach.

I remember how, right in the middle of the ceremony, a rawhide-bottomed chair cracked and went suddenly to pieces under Uncle Wiley and how he spent a full minute, it seemed like, grunting and straining and stomping and waving his arms around, trying to keep his balance. And how, in the dead silence that followed his finally sprawling full-length in the middle of the floor, Sis said "I do!" in such a strong and eager voice that it made her blush and everybody else laugh out loud. Only they pretended it was Uncle Wiley's mishap they were laughing at.

I remember how, just the minute the preacher said "I now pronounce you man and wife," Aunt Minnie broke out with a loud crying, like maybe Sis had just died, and ran up and grabbed Ruel Mac-

Laurin by both shoulders and started shaking him as fiercely as she sometimes shook Jay when he'd made her mad about something.

"Now, you be good to my honey girl," she said frantically, and then went to threatening Ruel. "If ever I learn that you've made her cry one time, I'll come after you with her papa's gun. And I'll use it, too. You understand?"

And she kept crying and shaking Ruel and threatening to shoot him till finally Uncle Ike had to come and pull her loose.

"Now, hush it up, Minnie," he ordered. "Our girl's just married the finest young man in the country, and we've got a right to be proud. But the sort of happy crying spells you pull off is liable to scare him clean out of the country."

And then, about the time the wedding dance was getting in full swing, I remember how Aunt Millie Creech went tearing all through the house, screaming at the top of her voice.

One of her babies was lost. She couldn't find it anywhere. It was the littlest one, the thumb-sucker that had got stuck under the floor the time we lost Uncle Wiley's toes.

Aunt Millie was frantic. Anything might have happened to that baby. Anything on earth. He might have fallen into a well. He might have wandered out into the lots and got eaten by a hog. He might have been kicked to death by a horse. He might have fallen off the roof of the house and be lying out in the dark, right now, with his little neck broken.

Before Aunt Millie could get through listing all the things that might have happened to her baby, Grandma Elfie led her into the kitchen and told her to look in the meal barrel while she held the light.

And, sure enough, there was Aunt Millie's thumb-sucker, bedded down in the corn meal with my pet possum Scott Cooley. Both of them fast asleep.

Grandma Elfie said she didn't know why it was, but any time you left the lid off a corn-meal barrel for any length of time, you could look to find a dog or a youngun or a housecat curled up on the meal, sleeping away.

What puzzled me so was how Scott Cooley had got to the wedding, in the first place. I sure hadn't thought to bring him.

But the thing I remember most about Sis's wedding is what Aaron Blood did that night. It was such an unexpected act, so heart-warming yet so disturbing in its implications, that telling about it now fills me with a certain shame that we ever allowed anybody to live along Recollection Creek in such terrible loneliness.

Blood didn't come to the wedding proper. He didn't arrive, in fact, until the dancing had reached the hollering and floor-stomping stage.

When a grown-up party reaches that rowdy peak of hilarity, kids my age generally get to feeling uneasy, sometimes even a little scared, and are likely to feel safer outside in the dark than inside underfoot. So Jay and I were sitting out on the front steps of Grandma's house, silent and sober at the thought of Jay's moving away the next day, when Aaron Blood rode into the lamplight that spilled out through the windows. He was riding his roan bull and leading a couple of saddled horses.

We didn't really pay any attention to him. We just watched him tie up his bull and the horses, mostly because we were sitting and looking in that direction. We didn't even speak to him till he came up and stood over us, as if hopeful for some sort of recognition. Then we said, "Howdy, Mr. Blood," and waited for him to go inside.

But he didn't. He stood there, looking red-faced and uncomfortable till he'd taken his hat off and wiped the sweat out of the inside with his handkerchief and gone to all the trouble of getting it set back on his head again. Then he said to Jay: "Being's you're leaving tomorrow, I figured it best to bring over the presents I got for you boys tonight."

I looked up at him, puzzled. "Presents?" I said.

He pointed his thumb back over his shoulder. "Them horses," he said. "I figured the black one for Jay and the bay for you. Course, if you want to swap, it ain't no consarn of mine."

Beside me, Jay came suddenly to his feet. He said in astonishment: "You mean, Mr. Blood, that you aim to give us them horses? Just flat-out *give* them to us?"

I jumped up then and stared wordlessly at Aaron Blood.

He wouldn't look at me. He wouldn't look at Jay, either. He just stood with his face getting redder by the second, looking at some point between and behind the two of us.

Finally, he said, in a sort of fierce anger: "Well, it's all right, ain't it? Ain't nothing to get mad about, is it? I figured you boys for my friends, and I don't see nothing wrong with giving a friend a present of some sort."

I got my breath then and said, "Gee whiz, Mr.

Blood!" and Jay said, "Goshamighty!" and led me in a fast run through the yard gate to get a closer look at the horses.

We brought them into the yard, where we could get a good look at them in the lamplight. Both were dandies. Both were proud steppers, as sleek and trim and clean-cut as any horse in the country. And both sporting new saddles stamped with rosebud patterns. As fancy as the saddle Ruel MacLaurin or Shiner Maverick rode.

The best I recollect, we never did actually get around to thanking Aaron Blood. Boys our age generally don't have the right words to thank gods for their gifts. Then, too, we were so excited and busy mounting and riding the horses around in the yard and making plans about how we'd enter them in the next horse race and win some money that we forgot. We'd grow up and become cowhands and wear high-heeled boots and silver-mounted spurs and bullhide chaps and rope wild cattle out of the brush and start us a ranch and hire Aaron Blood to be our foreman.

I guess that sort of talk was thanks aplenty for Aaron Blood. Anyhow, he stood leaning against a gallery post, with a crooked smile on his thick lips and a sort of misty shine in his eyes, till we ran out

of talk. Then he grunted a short good-by and went and straddled his roan bull and rode off into the dark.

And it wasn't till I ran into the house and dragged Papa out to show him my horse that I thought to question Blood's motives.

Or, rather, it was Papa who questioned them. Papa said right off that there was a catch to it somewhere and he went and got Uncle Ike, so they could talk it over and decide what to do.

Uncle Ike agreed with Papa. He was convinced that nobody would just up and buy a couple of knot-head kids a horse and saddle apiece, without he had in mind putting over something underhanded on somebody.

Uncle Ike told Papa they had better investigate the matter right away, before Blood caught one or both of them in some sort of squeeze they couldn't get out of. He said he couldn't hardly get away from the wedding party right then, but if Papa would, he might ought to follow Aaron Blood home and see if he could learn what it was all about.

The saddle on Jay's horse was too little for Papa to ride in, so he stripped it off and mounted the black bareback. I didn't want to go with him and told Papa so, but he made me go anyhow. He said he'd heard my side of the story and now he wanted to hear Blood's side of it, with me there listening.

Papa was like that. When he didn't understand something, he wouldn't leave a thing uncovered till he'd got the straight of it. All along that ride to Aaron Blood's house, I could feel him studying me in the dark, like he half-suspected that I'd lied to him about the whole thing.

Yellow lamplight shone through the open door of Blood's two-room shack when we rode up. Before Papa had time to holler a hello-the-house, Blood's stout silhouette filled the doorway.

"Who is it?" he demanded belligerently, and we saw him reach up and lift down a rifle from above the door.

"It's me, Blood," Papa said quickly. "Emil Creech. I've come to find out about this horse and saddle my boy claims you give him."

"All right," Blood said harshly. "I give it to him. What about it?"

That seemed to stump Papa. He sat silent on Jay's black horse for a good long while before he finally said: "Well, look, Blood. You can't afford to go around giving away good horses and saddles to boys. What's on your mind? What are you after?"

I was glad it was dark and nobody could see the

slow hot flush of burning shame that I could feel crawling up my neck and into my face right then.

I saw Blood's silhouette stiffen. When he spoke, it was in that tone of voice he always used with other grown people. The harsh, raspy, unyielding kind that grates on your nerves like scraping a rusty tin bucket with your fingernails.

"Well, Emil Creech," he said, "let me tell you something. I can afford to do whatever I please with my money. I give them horses to them boys because I like 'em. I like 'em because they treat me like I was somebody and don't ask no questions. Which is more than I can say for you or anybody else around in this country.

"On top of that, I was a youngun once and I done some hoping and dreaming, just like them boys. You was a boy once and you done the same thing. And now look at us. Me, a crabby old fool, too soured out with life for the good Lord hisself to get along with. You, greedy as a hog and trying to git your hands on every piece of land in the country. So greedy and suspicious you can't let a man give your boy a present without looking for some meanness behind it."

I could tell Papa was getting fighting mad by the way he slid suddenly off the horse and started toward Blood. But he didn't get three steps before Blood stopped him. Blood levered a shell into the barrel of his Winchester and told Papa to stand where he was, that he wasn't done with his speech-making yet.

"Now, it ain't right, Emil Creech," he went on, "for a boy to starve for things he wants so long that by the time he's growed up, he's all warped and twisted, like you and me. He ought to git some few of the things he aches for before it's too late."

I could see Papa shaking all over, and he took another step forward, then held it again. That was because Blood had lifted his Winchester and thumbed back the hammer.

"Just hold it, Emil Creech," he cautioned. "There ain't much more, but it's important, and I aim for you to hear it. . . . Now, when I give them horses to Hopper and Jay, I done it to make certain two kids I knowed wouldn't have to waste their whole lives wanting. And I still aim to make certain they don't. You do ary thing to keep Jay and Hopper from getting pleasure out of them horses, and you'll have me to deal with. And you can tell your brother Ike the same goes for him."

He stepped back a little ways from the door, then added: "And now that's all, and you can get back on that horse and git off my place. And make a hurry-up job of it!"

He slammed the door shut in our faces then, and I could hear him walking the floor till Papa finally mounted the black horse, and we rode away.

I don't think Papa ever did quite get it through his head what Aaron Blood was trying to say that night. And, at the time, I don't guess I did.

But I think I know now. I'm pretty certain he was trying to say the same thing that Grandma Elfie meant by her saying—that, generally, there is a period in everyone's life when he is more himself than at any other time between birth and death.

Only I don't think he'd been as lucky as Jay and I. I don't think that ever in his life Aaron Blood had known that wild, free, and irresponsible time when he actually felt really and truly *himself*.